Interplanetary Evil

As Moon Base Alpha is drawn inexorably off course by an intense and inexplicable gravitation force, the Alphans are compelled to contend with hazards that menace their survival as much as the ever-diminishing supply of Tirenium, essential to their life-support system:

- A computer with aspirations to immortality.

- Two members of an ancient stellar traveling race who bear the dreaded Mark of Achanon.

- A half-crazed man driven by the imminent destruction of the Moon Base that he has glimpsed in a vision.

- A race of rebellious androids who want to provoke the Alphans to hate and murder, so that they can be programmed to duplicate the evil.

Books In This Series

Space 1999 #1: Planets of Peril
Space 1999 #2: Mind-Breaks of Space

Published by
WARNER BOOKS

YEAR 2

SPACE 1999
#2
MIND-BREAKS
OF SPACE

BY MICHAEL BUTTERWORTH
Based on the dialogue and ideas of:
JACK RONDER   LEW SCHWARTZ
ANTHONY TERPILOFF   TONY BARWICK
—who wrote the original A.T.V. scripts for
Gerry Anderson Productions Ltd.,
Pinewood Studios.

WARNER BOOKS

A Warner Communications Company

WARNER BOOKS EDITION

Copyright © 1977 by ITC Incorporated Television Company Ltd. and Warner Books, Inc.

ISBN 0-446-88342-5

Photograph section designed by Marsha Gold

Warner Books, Inc., 75 Rockefeller Plaza, New York, N.Y. 10019

Printed in the United States of America

Not associated with Warner Press, Inc. of Anderson, Indiana

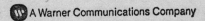A Warner Communications Company

First Printing: April, 1977

10   9   8   7   6   5   4   3   2   1

CHAPTER ONE

It hit them from out of nowhere.

The moment was so unexpected and so sudden that even Commander John Koenig himself was stunned into inaction. He could only stand and stare in amazement with the rest of the Command Center personnel as the warning letters flashed up on the Big Screen:

CHANGE OF HORIZON

and as the slow, certain flicking of the digits below told the progress of the alarming event:

0:01°, 0.02°, 0.03°, 0.04° ...

"John?" questioned Tony Verdeschi urgently, "what in God's name . . . ? We're changing course!"

The Security Chief's words broke the spell of shock. "I see it, Tony," Koenig said. "I don't understand it, but I see it." He glanced urgently over his shoulder. "Yasko," he ordered, "show me the horizon."

The attractive Japanese computer operator punched a new set of instructions for the computer.

Abruptly, the gray blankness—against which the coded computer data of the past three years had been flashing all that had been collected since the Moon had blasted free of its Earth orbit—began to clear.

The Moon Base had been taking advantage of a peaceful and uneventful month to transfer the valuable information it had gleaned during its unwilling and hazardous flight through space into the Main Computer Memory—a long-postponed operation that would greatly increase their chances of survival. But the operation had been abruptly halted by the arrival of the unexpected information. The mood of momentary calm, almost holiday-like, has been shattered in seconds.

An instrument display of the horizon flashed on the screen just above where it now said, CHANGE OF HORIZON 2.00°, and Koenig felt an icy chill of dread as the points of the gyroscopic gauge rolled slowly and steadily to the right from the constant zero.

Some stupendous force was acting on the Moon, drawing it inexorably toward . . . toward what?

"Maya!" he called out, keeping his eyes on the baffling figures. "What's pulling at us?"

Maya's Psychon eyes tensed with the seriousness of the moment. She let her fingers dance like lightning over the keyboard of her computer link. The small screen of the console in front of her immediately responded with a pearl-bright string of unhelpful zeros. That was the sensor's way of saying that no news may not be good news but for the moment that was all it had in stock.

"I have no reading, John," Maya reported worriedly.

"Yasko," Koenig ordered, "find something on the screen. Let's see what it looks like."

Yasko responded, and the puzzling information on the Big Screen vanished to be replaced by the black velvet of space and the cast diamonds across it of millions of stars. Vainly, all eyes in the Command Center searched for the single significant point that would explain this mysterious force.

Tony Verdeschi felt his quick-fired blood rage with impatience. He could deal with problems, but when their causes refused to come out and show themselves, he saw red. "It looks just the same as it always does!" he snapped.

"What factor could be involved in a change of course that we couldn't read?" Koenig asked Maya.

"Just one. A gravity pull from space," she replied.

He nodded, tight-lipped, then directed, "See if you can locate the source."

Immediately Maya and Yasko leaned across their consoles and began to send out directions to the intricate sensory monitors that formed the complex system of the Alpha Base's "eyes and ears." Coded lights danced across the cathode tubes.

"Predicted position of gravity source," Maya reported to Koenig and the rest of the waiting crew, "*no* prediction . . ." Her brow crinkled in astonishment.

"It doesn't make sense," Tony commented, verifying the computer's message on the ribbon of tape which chattered from the print-out. He shook his head with annoyance.

Koenig considered the situation for a moment, then ordered: "Give me a three-sixty-degree visual scan."

As he spoke, the powerful lens on the Moon's surface above the Command Center was brought into action. It swivelled slowly around and took in the complete dome of the galaxy ahead of them. Still nothing appeared that had the slightest significance to the mysterious grip of gravity that had captured them.

The horizon reading slipped noisily from 9.00° to 10.00° to 11.00°.

"John," Tony said tensely, stepping close to the Commander and keeping his voice down, "what if it's a black dwarf?"

Dr. Helena Russell was standing near enough to hear the question. She had placed herself instinctively close to Koenig when the emergency began, but to one side so as not to distract him from his handling of the situation. Only when she heard Tony's suggestion she reached out and gripped his arm.

"If we're going to collide with a black dwarf . . ." she began, frightened but also keeping her voice low so as not to spread alarm.

Koenig looked at her, sending a message of comfort Tony leaped to the big red switch and clicked it home. and regret with his eyes. He turned back to face Tony.

"Evacuation procedure!" he ordered firmly. "And fast!"

7

Tony leaped to the big red switch and clicked it home. Instantly the scream of the alert klaxon began to fill the corridors of the entire Moon Base complex. Tony leaned down to the microphone and connected himself to the speakers in the pilot's quarters. "All Eagles prepare to evacuate . . . prepare to evacuate!"

Helena switched herself through to the Medical Section. "Medical Section prepare to evacuate," she ordered, confirming the signal that would be flashing through the hospital already.

Koenig watched the monitor carefully to assess the rate of course change, wondering just how much time they had left. At last the carefully chosen few among all the personnel who could be taken off by the limited Eagle fleet were ready for the final order.

CHANGE OF HORIZON, 17.00°, the Big Screen flashed.

"Rate of change still constant," Maya reported. But suddenly she leaned forward in alarm. She stared at the figures. "But the rate of *close* is accelerating!"

Tony confirmed the bad news. "We're getting closer to whatever it is that's pulling us. We don't have much time."

Grimly, Koenig gave the only order he could, the one that might be his last. "Evacuate," he said tonelessly.

Across the Big Screen they watched the Eagle ships lift and soar toward some possibility of survival. It was a gesture rather like dropping lifeboats down in the middle of the ocean back on Earth, only there they could hope for reaching an island or rescue by a passing vessel. In the deep of space, the Eagle ships would have slim hope of either.

Then, as they watched, they noticed a tiny point of light which somehow stood out against all the sparkles in space.

It was a glassy, sinister, pulsating light.

"Focus and magnify!" Koenig ordered, starting forward.

The light shifted to the center of the screen and grew startlingly in size as the telescopic lens zoomed in on it.

8

It became a glowing ball masked with a swath of orange cloud.

"Identify!" he requested.

He was perplexed as Maya replied, "Estimates only."

"Estimates *only*?" he repeated, incredulously. "Why isn't our computer dealing with that?"

Tony provided the answer from his own circuit check. "It seems to have slowed up," he said, gritting his teeth.

Maya and Koenig both exchanged astounded glances. But it was a problem that would have to be gone into later, *if* there was a later. Koenig returned his attention to the planet ahead of them.

"Is that what's pulling us off course?" he asked.

"No, John," said Maya. "I calculate it's a small planet with no more gravity pull than we have."

Koenig's perplexity increased a hundredfold as suddenly into view on the screen flashed an unknown spaceship.

"What in—!" Tony gasped.

Koenig's surprise was compounded by the strange sensation that he had seen the spaceship, or one like it, before. It was certainly no Eagle, being smaller and sleeker, but there were certain touches that were oddly familiar. He put aside the thought for the moment and ordered, "Intercept the ship!"

Tony punched channels through to the Eagle flight and instructed Eagles One and Two to break off from the evacuation formation.

A moment later the amplified voice of the Eagle One pilot came back over the speakers. "Eagle One to Moon Base. We now have visual contact."

Koenig switched himself through to the pilot on his own monitor. "Command Center to Eagle One," he identified. "Are you having any abnormal gravity from that spaceship?"

"No, John. Gravity is normal."

Koenig settled back thoughtfully, shaking his head. He listened as the Eagles maneuvered into interception positions. They had no difficulty, since the alien spaceship continued imperturbably along its course toward the

Moon, taking no evasive action. He watched Eagle One abruptly swerve in toward the ship with a blast of thrust rockets to close on it.

"Eagle One to spaceship," the pilot's voice sounded across the speakers as he tried to make contact. "Eagle One to spaceship. Do you receive me?" There was silence while everyone listened with bated breath. "We are friendly," the Eagle pilot added as an afterthought.

They waited tensely, half assuming the ship to carry no life. Out of the grave-like stillness came a reply. It was a ringing, youthful voice, and it surprised them all.

"Hello, Eagle One!" it greeted. "Am I glad to hear you! Eagles from planet Earth, good old merry terry firma! WA-OW! And is that, or is that not, the dear old Moony-moon-moon?"

The Eagle pilot was just as dumbfounded as the Command personnel. It almost seemed like some incredible practical joke. He hesitated just on that point, not wanting to be made the butt of a prank. Then he thought again and knew that what he had just heard was real enough and it was his responsibility to return the communication.

"Eagle One to spaceship. That *is* the Moon." He took a deep breath and added the standard request. "Please identify yourself."

"Hello, Eagle!" The voice seemed not to have heard them. It had its own version of communications routine. "How are ya? My spaceship is a Swift, also originating from Earth."

Of course, thought Koenig as soon as he heard it. The Swift was an earlier model of the Eagle ships, especially designed for deep space exploration. But it couldn't have come this far from Earth by itself. Swifts were support vessels for larger mother ships.

He didn't have to ask as the bubbly, informal voice explained, "I was on a star mission, with three other Swifts and a mother ship. We left Earth in nineteen ninety-six."

Instantly Koenig ordered a computer check. This time there didn't seem to be any slowness in the response, and the answer flickered up brightly on Maya's screen.

"Star mission in nineteen ninety-six," she confirmed. "Mother ship and four Swifts. Under the command of a Captain Michael."

"What happened to them?"

Maya had the answer ready. "Communication break. Fate unknown."

Koenig considered this while he watched the Eagle maneuver closer to the Swift. In the meantime they had both, along with Eagle Two, drawn much closer to the Moon.

"Say, bird baby," the Swift's mysterious voice quipped, "there used to be a base on the Moon. What was it . . . um, Alpha? Is it still there? Is it manned?"

The Eagle pilot confirmed, "Moon Base Alpha is operational."

The words brought back the state of the crisis to Koenig. Logic told him that any unusual gravitational effects should have been overwhelmingly apparent to the Eagles and to the Swift in front of them. Yet they obviously weren't aware of any.

"We might be more operational if we knew more about that gravity pull." He shot a questioning glance at Maya, "Do we have any more data?"

"No, sir. The force registering on the monitor seems to have stabilized. I'll check and see if I can determine whether there is a real gravity threat, or if our computer has developed a fault."

Koenig started to ask the probability of such a thing's happening when his attention was diverted by the voice from the Swift booming through the Command Center speakers.

"Swift to Alpha . . . hi, big Alpha! Boy, oh boy, listen, you guys . . ." Helena almost laughed at the familiarity. "I ain't seen or heard no one for so long I'd just about given up." Tony didn't quite know how to take the informality, being still wrought up about the catastrophe that had seemed imminent only minutes before. "Hey, there!" the voice yelled. "Can I come down and have lunch with you?"

Koenig gave himself a moment to consider carefully, then put his microphone through to the open channel. "Moon Base Alpha to Swift. Come on down and have lunch with us." He carefully closed the channel before turning and giving Tony a meaningful nod.

Tony tuned in a special frequency on his transmitter. "Weapons Section," he said confidentially. "Lasers on standby. Target—incoming spaceship, Swift class. Range—five hundred kilometers."

A steady, businesslike voice replied, "Weapons Section acknowledges Command Center. Defense System activated and standing by."

Tony fed the Swift's coordinates into the automatic tracking system for the lasers and pressed the "Armed" button so that Koenig could see on his control board that everything was prepared. All the Commander had to do was press the "Fire" button and the Swift would be ripped to scrap metal.

Both Eagles took up escort positions alongside the Swift as it dropped down toward Alpha, but maintained a reasonablie distance from it. They knew fully well what precautions Koenig would take. As the Swift swooped down to a landing pad and settled gently with its braking rockets, the Eagles hovered above, keeping a precautionary watchful eye.

"Helena," Koenig said, moving toward the Command Center doors, "would you like to join the reception committee?"

Two Security guards met them at the entrance to the travel tube that had extended and secured itself to the airlock of the Swift. Each of them cradled a stun-gun over one arm and looked purposefully serious. They both had wariness and nerveless professionalism drilled into them when they had attended the Flight Security School back on Earth. It was an occupational polish that Koenig had encouraged in them as well as in all the other skills and trades that were practiced by the three hundred people on the Moon Base. He returned their familiar salute and led the way into the travel tube. It shot away toward the ship.

He was only a stride away from the airlock doors of the Swift when they slid open with a gentle gush of air. Inside he could see the dimly lit and vaguely familiar design of the passenger section. There were not many differences between it and the Eagle interiors, apart from the slightly overpowering lavender upholstery, which immediately caught Helena's eye.

"This is the Commander of Moon Base Alpha," Koenig announced loudly. "We're coming aboard."

There was no answer.

The security guards had more on their minds than the décor as they slipped the safety catches on their guns and moved cautiously inside. The passenger section was empty and showed no evidence of being recently used at all. The Lieutenant stepped quickly across to the door to the pilot section. The other guard held his gun at the ready as the door opened.

Jumping into the cabin, the Lieutenant's eyes raced from one empty seat to the other. Pilot, Co-Pilot and Navigator . . . there was no one there. The cockpit was as vacant and silent as a robbed tomb.

Back in the travel tube the Lieutenant reported, extremely puzzled, "There's no one there, sir."

Koenig was no less puzzled himself and decided it would be safest to withdraw quickly. "Okay, Lieutenant," he said, "let's go back."

"Just no sign of anyone sir."

"Is it in good order—there's no indication of anything unusual?"

The security man shook his head. "Not that I can tell. It's just empty."

From inside the Swift's still open door the voice came loud and clear. "Okay, fellers, okay. You've had your inspection." All the Alphans turned in amazement. "You're well armed, I see. Good thinking. Anyhow, I get the fact that you really are from Earth, so that's okay. We're all friends."

"Where are you?" the Lieutenant blurted out.

13

"Just coming. Where's your Commander?"

"I'm here," Koenig replied.

"What's your name?"

Koenig looked across at Helena, wondering whether the continued casual attitude to protocol was a result of such long isolation in space. "Koenig," he said.

Helena ventured a question of her own. "And what's your name?"

"Oh, lady, what a question! *I* don't have a name. Just wait a second and I'll meet you there."

The security men had their guns at the ready once again but as they looked into the Swift's airlock, they lowered them slowly in confusion. Filling the entranceway was a rectangular cabinet about four feet high. It rolled forward on hidden wheels, and the lights and dials on its front blinked and wiggled according to the flow of power inside it. On its top a triple-lensed video scanner played back and forth across the welcoming group and a large amber tube flared in brightness according to the pattern of its speech.

"Koenig?" the voice they knew well by then asked, and the amber blipped once.

Koenig raised his hand slightly. "That's me."

"Pleased to meetcha." The lens swung across to Helena. "And you're the lady."

"I'm Doctor Russell."

"How are ya, Doctor Russell? Would you like to show me around your lovely little Moon Base now?"

The cabinet rolled forward steadily and surely, like visiting royalty. Suddenly it stopped. "Say," it asked, "there aren't any steps or stairs, are there? See, I'm on wheels and I can't cope with bumps, you know? Didn't think of that when they made me. And hey, you guys, watch my antenna." The box swerved slightly to draw attention to the short strip of metal that hung from the back and dragged on the floor. "I'd better tell you what's what, huh? Who I am, I mean."

Koenig felt slightly wary, in spite of a certain sense of amusement at the incredible machine. "Yes," he agreed. "*Who* are you?"

14

"Like I said, Star Mission Nineteen Ninety-Six. Our mother ship and the other Swifts landed on a planet that's quite close by. We called it Planet D." Koenig could swear there was a plaintive note of sorrow in the box's voice as it added, "And they died, all of them, they just died. I've been orbiting ever since, waiting for another Earth mission to turn up."

Helena, too, heard the tremor of sadness and in spite of her scientist's certainty that machines couldn't feel emotion, felt a twinge of sympathy. "Were you part of the original . . . uh . . . crew?" she asked.

"I'm a rolling, talking seeing head, a beautiful boogie brain for that old computer on the Swift. It provides the energy and stores the data, and *I* do the thinking. My antenna lets me move around while still keeping in contact with my body, so to speak."

In shifting aside for another nervous look at the box's tail, the Lieutenant accidentally brushed his foot over the end of it. The lights and dials on the front suddenly went crazy, blipping and jerking.

"Ye-oww!" he shouted. "Don't step on it, it gives me the heebie-jeebies. Not to mention a headache!"

The Lieutenant stepped back guiltily. "Sorry . . ."

Koenig felt edgy uncertainty, and there was just the hint of a question he felt he should ask. Exactly what it was eluded him, so he queried instead, "What can we call you?"

The box seemed to have calmed down quickly. "Well, like I said, I ain't got no name. There's only one of me, so I don't need a name, do I?"

"You called yourself The Brain before . . ."

"That's not my name, that's what I am. Actually, pal, the first word I ever said was Brain, only I got it wrong. I said Brian. That's a name, so if you wanna call me something I reckon that would do. Just call me Brian."

That at least settled, Koenig gave the order to return them to the base, and the travel tube speeded quickly on its way. Brian thought the vacuum-propelled tube idea was terrific and suggested it would be fun to ride up and down in one all day long.

"By the way," Koenig asked Brian as they moved through a corridor toward the Command Center. "We've registered a change of course for the Moon. Rather a severe one. Has your computer . . . have *you* any data on that?"

"No, I haven't," Brian said with a credulous blinking of his amber light. "What d'you mean, change of course . . . what's pulling you?"

"That's what we're trying to find out," Helena explained.

"You mean a gravity pull? Like from Planet D? A collision course for Planet D wouldn't be very funny. Gee, I'll check on that."

Inside the Command Center Tony, Maya, and Yasko waited anxiously for the Commander and Helena to return. Tony had already ordered the evacuation to be aborted and the ships to return to the base.

Maya had become increasingly concerned about the reliability of the base computer. Its response to routine procedure was still fitful and sluggish, a difficulty she had never had before.

She looked up perfunctorily as Koenig came in through the main doors. She was waiting for the results of a test program she had put in. Then, as she realized what else her glance had taken in, she looked up again in astonishment.

Brian was rolling in, his panel lights rippling with curiosity. "Hi, folks! How are ya?" His video lens was jerking brightly from side to side. "I'm fine, just okey-dokey. Real nice to see you all. I thought I was going to be stuck here twiddling my thumbs for a century or two."

Yasko was away from her console, checking through the replacement circuits on the top of a maintenance trolley that Maya had asked for. Brian came scooting right across to her, and her kittenish Oriental eyes widened.

"Say, chick, what's your name?"

"Y-Y-Yasko."

"I think you're pretty cute, Yasko, what are you doing

16

tonight? Hahaha. Just kiddin'...but say," he rolled slowly around the maintenance trolley, viewing its gleaming chrome, "I really could go for your friend here. Just dig those yellow plastic wheels, will you!" He surprised them all with a very accurate and loud wolf whistle.

No one spoke for a confused moment, then Brian burst out laughing, his amber light flashing like mad. "Hahaha. Just kiddin', fellas. That trolley don't mean nothing to me...hahaha. Yellow wheels, my foot!"

Helena found she couldn't resist the humor, and Koenig was having a hard time keeping his face straight, as well. Only Maya seemed impervious to the joviality. She had too much on her mind about the computer's erratic functioning, and perhaps that was why she felt an extra twinge of anxiety as Brian rolled right up to the computer's input banks.

"Hey," he said, "your computer's the same as mine. Mark Ten Holographic Programming, yeah? Him and me, we're compatible, only he don't talk...voice-wise." Brian suddenly emitted a series of short sharp whistles and resonant bleeps, his front panel lights fluttering. The monitor lights on the input bank of the base's computer flashed off and on in response several times. Maya felt an inexplicable dread as she watched. "Haha," Brian laughed, turning around, "that was just a quick hello in computer talk. I feel sorry for the poor guy, you know, he's never been born."

"Well," said Koenig, trying to be hospitable, "I'd offer you that lunch you asked for, but I don't know what we've got that you'd like."

"Naw, I was just being sociable. I don't have no digestive system, man. A couple of kilowatts keeps me going real nice." Brian began to roll toward the center doors. "Listen, I'll get back and check that change of course now. Doc Russell, if you've got a moment, I'd like to give you a tour of my humble abode and also ask you some questions about the death of my crew..." the voice paused reverently, "and the Captain. Maybe you can help figure out the causes."

Helena nodded readily. "I'd be glad to be of help."

"Do you mind if I come along?" asked Koenig, interested himself in discovering the fate of the Star Mission. There was a chance it had some bearing on the day's unusual events.

"Mind? Why should I mind? I'm delighted you want to come."

After they had gone, Tony walked across to watch Maya prepare another test to run through their computer. "What did you make of that? What the hell was it?"

Maya frowned. "Some kind of mobile, self-programming computer. Self-monitoring, too."

"That sounds like it's alive?"

"That depends on how you define life. It doesn't breathe, eat, or reproduce. But it certainly seems to think for itself." Maya reached out and gripped Tony's hand. "I don't know why, Tony, but I have a bad feeling about that machine."

"A bad *feeling*?" Tony smiled indulgently. "Come on, Maya, give it a chance. It's doing a check for us, and since we can't seem to find out where we're heading, that will be very helpful." He squeezed her hand, enjoying the contact. "Actually, it's made my day, that silly box. You're just jealous because your brain works so much like a computer you're worried about competition."

Maya ignored the lighthearted jibe. "I still think something's wrong. Open a channel to the Swift and let's see what they're doing."

Tony crossed over to the communications board and hit a button. The monitor screen which had been holding the horizon-change information went blank and should have replaced the image with the Swift's interior. Instead it stayed dead gray.

Tony punched the button again, but there was no change. Anxiously Maya leaned over her own controls and tapped out a query for the ailing computer. There was no response.

There was a moment's horrified silence, and then Maya leaped to her feet and rushed across to the Red Alert button and slapped her hand down on it.

18

"You have no authority to do that!" Tony shouted angrily. "Only the Commander can order a Red Alert, or in his absence, me!"

Maya simply faced him impatiently, waiting for him to catch on. Tony stopped his tirade and looked at the base communications monitors. There was not a sound or a flicker of a response. The alert system was dead as well.

"We've been cut off!" Tony shouted to Yasko. "Get somebody to bring the Commander and Doctor Russell back here immediately!"

At that moment there was just the slightest tremor in the floor of the unusually quiet Command Center. They would never have noticed it under normal operating conditions, but now they did, and sure as anything, they knew it was the Swift blasting off.

CHAPTER TWO

John Koenig was pitched across the passenger compartment and crashed heavily into the padded bulkhead. The sudden blast-off had caught him and Helena by surprise, only she had been lucky enough to fall backwards into one of the seats. Koenig looked up with a spinning sensation behind his eyes and saw Brian rocking precariously back and forth on its wheels, but managing to stay upright.

"Sorry folks, sorry," he announced. "We took off a little quickly. Now don't panic me, or we'll all be in trouble. Just leave me be till I get this ship under control."

Koenig ignored the request and angrily demanded, "What do you think you're doing? I insist that—"

"Shut up!" Brian barked.

Koenig and Helena were both taken off guard by the change of character of the machine. Then Koenig felt his indignation welling up again. As the color rose in his face, Helena lifted an admonishing hand.

"Remember, John, it's only a machine."

Koenig ignored her and pulled himself up to his feet, making Brian roll back to get out of his way. Suddenly the Swift tilted radically and Koenig tripped backwards.

"Ohhh," wailed Brian, "I told you! Will you just sit down and get your belts on a minute? I'll ramble up to the flight deck and get everything shipshape."

Koenig watched it roll through the doorway into the pilot section, then scrambled across to Helena. "Are you all right?" he asked.

She nodded, but Brian seemed to have heard the question as well and shouted back, "Yeah, I'm all right. I sure as heck better be!"

"I wasn't talking to you," Koenig said. "Where are you going?"

The voice almost snarled. "I'm going to my pilot console, I said! Pull yourself together, Koenig."

Koenig motioned for Helena to stay where she was and walked stealthily to the door of the pilot section. There was a steely seriousness in his dark eyes, the joking rapport now forgotten. He gripped his hand laser and held it in front of him.

Brian was concentrating fully on the ship's controls, checking out all the engine functions and the navigation program. Small bleeps of communication seemed to be passing back and forth between it and the control board as the tri-lens turned to look at the pilot's screen. Koenig could see it, too, and on it the glaring white surface of the Moon growing quickly smaller.

The tri-lens swung around to view Koenig just as Helena came up close behind him. "Uh-huh, Commander," Brian said, "just take it easy while I trim this course."

"Trim it back to Moon Base Alpha," Koenig ordered.

"Here's where we're heading," Brian stated flatly. The pilot's screen glazed over, and the view of the Moon was replaced by a telescopic close-up of the orange-clouded planet.

"Planet D?" asked Helena.

"You got it, lady." Without another word Brian turned and backed rapidly into a gap in the control panel. He became completely indistinguishable from the rest of the hardware, and Koenig could well understand how the security men had overlooked him.

Koenig moved carefully over to the pilot's seat, keeping his laser aimed at the section of machinery he knew was Brian. With his free hand he tried the controls, seeing if the ship would respond to a change of course.

Brian's voice said easily, "It's channelled through me, bud."

"Program this ship to return to Alpha." Koenig lifted the laser threateningly.

"If you fire that and destroy me, the airlocks will open and you and the lady will be swept into space." The tri-lens caught Helena glancing toward the lockers for the crew's spacesuits. "And if you make a move for those suits, I'll let the air out before your foot touches the ground. Now sit down!"

Helena hesitated, thinking about Brian's threat. It was true enough that he could slip open the airlocks and both she and John would be spat out into space like two apple pips. Brian didn't need air to keep functioning, so it—he—would be all right. Helena eased herself down in the Navigator's chair.

"Now, Commander," said Brian, a measure of superiority in his voice. "Put that gun down ... there on the shelf."

Koenig kept the weapon aimed at the center of the console. "Let me communicate with Alpha," he insisted.

"Of course I will, just put the gun down."

Koenig shook his head. "I don't trust you."

"Hard luck! Put your gun on the shelf or out you go ... and remember Koenig, I can't eject one of you without the other going as well. If you go, she goes. Ready? One . . . two . . ."

There was a sucking hiss of air. The astral charts near Helena began to lift upwards and a pen skidded across the panel top. Koenig looked around and saw Helena's face whiten with fear.

Leaning forward in the chair, he laid the laser on the narrow shelf. As soon as he moved his hand away, the shelf swung upward so that it and the laser disappeared into the shiny blue bulkhead. There was a loud click and the whoosh of the gun being jettisoned through some disposal system into space. The shelf dropped back into place, empty.

"Now then, Commander," said Brian gaily, "I'll give you service . . . not with a smile, 'cause I ain't got no face to smile with. But here's your service, all right."

Koenig and Helena both looked down at the pilot's viewscreen and saw an image cohere of the inside of Alpha's Command Center. Tony, Maya, and Yasko could be clearly seen . . . and so could the fact that something had gone badly wrong.

In the Command Center, unaware they were under observation, Tony and Maya worked desperately to try to restore the computer function. Maya attempted to get a straight line through to the Medical Center, but all she could raise on her screen was a wriggling slow line of random electrical current.

"Nothing but a mathematical sine wave . . . no matter what button I hit." She tried another channel, and another, with the same result. Her ultra-logical mind told her there was only one answer, but she refused to give up. "Tony, try the memory bank from your side. Ask it the date."

Tony coded in his query and got the same blind worm of a line on his screen. He tried asking the diameter of the Moon . . . the days since leaving Earth orbit . . . the number of personnel on the base. Only the sine wave fluttered before him.

Maya pushed her chair away and let her hands fall helplessly in her lap. "Either all the links to our computer have been blocked," she said, "or else its memory has been wiped clean. Either way, it's paralyzed."

"And so is the Moon Base," Tony pointed out, "and blind as well."

Maya got to her feet and pointed a trembling finger of accusation toward the sky. "It was that damn machine! It has the same computer link as we have. When it came in here, it gave an eradication command!"

The Command Center doors snapped open, and the pilot of Eagle One came striding in, looking worried. The expressions on the faces that greeted him didn't make him feel any better.

"What's going on?" he asked. "I've been sitting on the launch pad waiting to hear from you."

"Our communications have been wiped," explained Tony grimly. "All of them."

"Jeez!"

Maya had a sudden inspiration. "What about the computer on Eagle One? Is that all right?"

"Of course it is."

"Then what are we waiting for?" shouted Tony. "Let's get a squadron of Eagles together. The Commander and Doctor Russell have been abducted aboard that Swift. We've got to get them back."

Aboard the Swift itself, the screen suddenly cut off. Koenig looked across at Brian's tri-lens and saw the glimmer of amber in the tube below it signal that he was about to speak.

"That's a good crew, Koenig." The voice was bright with amusement. "You know what these boys of yours are showing? They're showing loyalty." Brian's cabinet rolled out a little way from the panel and back in again, as if it were doing a dance step. "Wa-hoo! I like it, I like it. I'll make a note of that!"

Without warning the pilot's screen came back on again. This time the view was a close-up of the Eagle pads near the base, and Eagles One, Two, Three, and Seven were blasting off. They lifted in a fast tight formation, flame gushing fiercely underneath them. It was a cheering sight to Koenig and Helena, but Brian didn't seem bothered.

"Hang on, folks," he warned. "I'm going to slow down."

Koenig wondered what the crazy little box planned to do next.

The pilot of Eagle One noticed that the Swift had fired its reverse rockets and seemed to be waiting for them to catch up. He pointed the fact out to Tony and Maya, who were standing anxiously behind his chair.

"It could be a trap," Tony suggested. "We'd better spread out and encircle it."

The other Eagles angled away and moved off to approach the Swift from different directions.

Tony was just about to order them to close in when he was surprised by Commander Koenig's grim face on the screen.

"Commander Koenig!" the pilot said in surprise.

"Pilot," ordered Koenig, "you will return to Moon Base."

"My information, sir, is that you and Doctor Russell are prisoners."

Koenig nodded brusquely. "That's so, but if you don't return to Moon Base right now, your computers will be blinded and then you won't be able to get back at all."

In the background Tony could make out the lively voice of that damn, smart-alec box yelling at Koenig. It said, "Tell them you're okay! I'll provide you with food and drink . . . whatever ya want. You want music . . . right, I got music!"

Koenig glanced off screen and then back at the pilot. "We're being . . . looked after," he said. "Now, acknowledge my command."

With great reluctance the pilot sighed and said, "Command received."

Tony leaned down to the screen before the contact was broken and asked quickly, "What is it that this mad, hijacking fruit machine wants, anyway?"

The voice of Brian came screaming through the receiver. "Fruit machine! Who are you calling a fruit machine, you pin-brained hairy meatloaf?"

Koenig interrupted before The Brain had a chance to do something rash. "Eagle One!" he barked. "Return to Moon Base. Immediately!"

The pilot acknowledged the order once again and reset the course to lead the other Eagles back to Alpha. Maya was thinking quickly, and a plan was taking shape. She would wait. When they had gone far enough away, the Swift's Brain would lose interest. Then she would make sure that they were protected from any radio eavesdropping. There might be a way to surprise that gaudy filing cabinet yet.

The Swift moved into an approach orbit for Planet D. The dull yellow clouds formed slow swirls below them, weakly reflecting the distant light of the system's sun. Koenig thought that it must not have been a very appealing sight for members of the Star Mission. They could have hardly expected to make more than a perfunctory exploration and never imagined their visit would last forever.

Helena, too, was thinking how unattractive the small planet looked. Probably it would not have been bothered with if not for the fact that it very obviously had an atmosphere. More than likely, the stopover had been at the instigation of the mission's astro-biologists to see if there were any specimens worth collecting.

"What's it like on the surface?" she asked Brian.

"Kinda like the Moon. Mostly dry surface . . . some ice."

"But it has air, an oxygen content?"

The Brain waited for a strangely long pause before answering. When it did, the voice had a forced note of casualness in it, a flavor of deception. "Yeah, yeah, it sure does. There's a kind of mist, though. Those orange clouds go right down to the surface, and they could be, you know, poisonous."

Helena looked nervously across at Koenig. He was weighing the information carefully himself, and Brian seemed to sense their suspicions. "Aw, come on, folks!" he shouted with forced liveliness. "Be happy, I've brought you together here. I can offer you all the time in the world. What more could you ask for—I mean, you love each other, don't you?"

Koenig shrewdly caught Helena's eye before replying, "No."

"Of course not," she said.

The panel lights down Brian's front rippled thoughtfully while he considered their denials. "Do you mind if I test that?" he asked. "I've got to be sure. We've got two airlocks in the passenger module. I want one of you in each."

"What if we don't choose to?" asked Koenig.

Brian didn't bother to answer; there was a low humming sound and the interior lighting composition of the spaceship began to change. The normal illumination dimmed as Brian increased the strength of the ultraviolet wavelength.

The force of the light glared until the cabin was saturated with it and Helena shrieked with pain.

"Shut your eyes!" shouted Koenig.

"That won't do you any good," laughed Brian. "I can turn it up until your eyeballs shrivel."

"Please turn it off," begged Helena.

"Will you get into the airlocks?"

"Yes, yes!" agreed Koenig. "Just turn this damn light off."

The purple light disappeared as the humming ceased and normal lighting was restored. Koenig quickly followed Helena through to the passenger section. They found the inner doors of the twin airlocks standing open, ready for them. Koenig hesitated but remembered the savage agony of the ultraviolet light and stepped inside the one on the right.

"That's fine, Koenig," said Brian from the doorway. He had followed them through. "Now you, lady, into the other one. Don't worry."

Helena set little store by the reassurance but stepped inside and turned around.

"Okay, good girl." Brian rolled backward and forward jauntily on his wheels. "Now I've really got to know

26

about you two. I just have to know." He rolled closer to the airlocks. "Koenig, do you love this lady?"

"No, I don't." Koenig stared straight-faced into the inquisitive tri-lens.

"Hmm, and Doctor Russell, do you love this man?"

She shook her head. "No, I told you I don't."

Suddenly transparent doors hissed closed across the airlocks, sealing them both. Koenig banged his hands angrily on the perspex. Brian's voice came sweetly through the speakers inside the separate airlocks.

"What I'm gonna do," he told them, "is let the air out slowly. Inside both airlocks you'll find a black button . . ." Koenig and Helena both saw the button set separately on a small panel of green and blue ones. "Now any time, folks, while the air is getting thinner, you can press your button and that will channel all your remaining air into the other airlock. You get it? If you press your button, Koenig, all the rest of your air goes to the lady. Doctor Russell, if you hit your black button, you give all your remaining air to Koenig, and he can live."

Helena was gripped with icy fear. "John!" she shouted at the dividing wall between the airlocks.

On his side Koenig was shouting, too. "Helena! Helena, can you hear me?"

The Brain's amused voice crackled through the speakers again. "I gotta tell you, you can't communicate with each other. No way, folks. Ready? Here goes."

Koenig and Helena both heard the snake-like sound as their supply began to slither out. At first it was as much from the psychological effect as the physical one that they began to feel the ache of suffocation.

Helena pounded her fists pointlessly on the clear panel. "Brian!" she shouted. "Let me talk to John!" She felt herself starting to pant.

Koenig, too, hammered at the wall, his eyes flicking desperately from the blank vision lens on top of The Brain to the panel on the wall with its neat black button. He could feel his lungs straining hard to draw in what was left of the precious air.

Brian looked back and forth to the scene in both

airlocks, reading the pleading desperation on Helena's face and the anger on Koenig's. In between he could see the dials that recorded the air level in each lock and the needles steadily sliding toward zero. Inside the airlocks Helena and John began to slide, too, their legs losing the strength to hold them up. Almost simultaneously their hands jerked up and punched down the black buttons.

"Wow-wee!" whooped Brian. "Both at the same time! You can have all your air back."

The delicious oxygen whooshed back into both airlocks, and when the pressure was equalized, Brian opened the panels and Helena and John both slumped weakly out to the floor.

"Folks, you love each other!" Brian announced triumphantly. "Golly, all I gotta do is keep one of you hostage and that gives me an eighteen-karat gold crunch on the other. Looks like I'm backing a winner!"

Koenig felt his blood boil as he raised his aching eyes and watched the hateful box roll back into the pilot section. He knew The Brain now had a pressure hold on them, but couldn't imagine how he was going to use it.

Brian guided the Swift in for a landing on Planet D without any trouble at all, simply putting the program from his first-ever visit into the guidance system. The vertical jets maneuvered the Swift steadily over the old landing site and let it down gently on the shock-absorbing pods.

Koenig watched the screen as external cameras played across the setting outside. He could make out very little detail through the constantly drifting orange mist. He disliked the idea of going out there by himself without any idea of what he might find. Brian refused to say anything more about what had happened to the Star Mission's crew, even though Koenig knew he must have more information.

Helena was even more worried than Koenig as she got one of the spacesuits out of the locker and checked that it was functioning properly. She had no idea why The Brain wanted John to go out there, but reasoned that there must be risks. Otherwise why hadn't The Brain simply gone himself?

At least the suit was in good order. All the controls were functioning, the temperature regulator was operating even though Brian had said that wouldn't be necessary, and the air supply was fully stocked. She wondered again what had been the fate of the man who once considered the suit his own and whether John was about to be forced to share it.

Koenig stepped across to her and took the suit out of her hands, carrying it back into the passenger module to put it on. Brian followed Helena as she joined Koenig and helped him to get dressed.

"Come on, come on, lady!" Brian was agitated. "Move faster."

Helena fumbled nervously with the fastenings. "I'm doing it as fast as I can."

"I don't believe you, lady . . . you're deliberately going slow." Brian was showing a glimmer of paranoid hysteria.

"Why are you making John go out there?" she asked angrily. "Why don't you go yourself?"

Brian seemed caught for an answer. He rolled up and down nervously on his wheels and his tri-lens swivelled around as though looking for a diversionary tactic. "Umm, well . . ." There was almost a pink blush in the hue of his amber vocal pattern light. "It's just . . . it's too bumpy out there. I told you I'm on wheels. I couldn't cross the terrain."

Koenig was finally into the suit. He ran a check of the controls himself and tested to see that the radio was working. Raising the helmet up and slipping it over his head, he locked it into place with the face plate still up.

"One thing you haven't told me," Koenig said as he stepped over to the airlock, "is why you want me to go out there at all. What is it you're after?"

"Yeah, right, Koenig, right. Well, the fact is we're landed about a hundred and fifty yards from my old mother ship. I want you to stroll on over there, unload the nuclear fuel store, and bring it back here and stick it in my storage tanks. Real simple, huh?"

Helena shook her head. "Why fuel? You must have enough nuclear fuel here. Enough for a thousand years."

"Enough!" Brian almost shrieked. "What the hell is a thousand years to me? There's enough fuel on that mother ship to last me a billion years! I'm gonna live forever!"

There was no conveniently welcoming travel tube for Koenig so he had to make his own way down the side of the Swift by a ladder. The surface was some thirty feet below him, lost in misty, ocher swirls.

As he descended, his mind was full of the final severe warning by the Brain not to try a double-cross. He had warmed up the ultraviolet light again, just enough to make Helena cry out in pain, as a grim reminder of what would happen otherwise. And of course the airlock test had given him an insight on how much Koenig would do to keep Helena safe.

As he went carefully down he kept glancing anxiously below him, trying to get a hint of what he was heading toward. He only wished Brian had been more willing to tell him exactly what the planet's conditions were like. There seemed to be enough heat trapped in the atmosphere to make it comfortable for human life, and according to the sensor reading on the spacesuit's life support system, there was a high enough oxygen content to even make the air breathable. In spite of that, Brian had insisted that he wear the suit and keep it fully functional. Therefore there must be another danger, a menace that wasn't immediately obvious . . . and which had claimed the lives of the entire Star Mission's crew.

Naturally enough, Brian wouldn't let Koenig get his hands on a weapon, so he had to come out unarmed. God only knew what was waiting for him down there, and by the time Koenig could see it, it would be too late. He cursed the encircling and unrelenting fog. If only he could see!

At last he could tell he was getting close to the ground. Now it was the underbody of the Swift that was lost from view, and he could make out the blue, jagged tips of rocks that rose up nearby. He reached out with one foot and tested for a firm foothold. The ground moved slightly and then firmed—the shifting feeling greatly similar to the dust on the Moon. He set the other foot down and turned slowly. So far, so good.

With great care he moved forward, sliding the well-padded shoes of the spacesuit along the soil to avoid stumbling over hidden rocks or holes as the mist thickened and wrapped around his knees.

He hadn't gone far when there was an abrupt clearing in the cloud, just a peculiar natural gap so that he could see clearly for several yards all around him. That was when he saw the first one.

"What is it, Koenig? What's the matter?" Brian's urgent voice throbbed through the earphones in the space helmet.

Koenig realized he must have involuntary gasped at the sight in front of him. It was one of the Star Mission crewmen. He was not wearing a spacesuit, so Koenig could see clearly the twisted and agonized expression that had been the last sensation of the man's life. The corpse was decaying slowly, and Koenig could see that it showed no signs of dying as a result of violence. Because of the lack of evidence that the body had been interfered with, even after death, Koenig deduced that there must not be much on Planet D in the way of animal life. And because of the low rate of decomposition, not much in the way of microorganisms, either.

"I've found one of the crewmen," Koenig said into the helmet's microphone. He had only gone two steps when he found another; like the first, he was not spacesuited, and he had died in an agony that seemed to have no exterior physical cause.

By the time Koenig had arrived at the mother ship he had passed over fifty bodies. All of them were in exactly the same condition.

CHAPTER THREE

Helena stared futilely at the screen, seeing nothing but the shroud of fog into which Koenig had disappeared. If the instructions of The Brain had been correct, he would soon be arriving at the mother ship . . . unless . . . She tried to force the fearful thought of the unknown danger from her mind.

"I wish we could see him," she said to Brian.

"Visibility is always a little on the low side on Planet D, lady," Brian told her, rolling alongside to peer at the monotonous view himself. "Don't worry. As long as he follows instructions, he'll be okay."

Helena looked around at the packing crate full of computer hardware and tried to reconcile what she could see with the bizarre, immortality-seeking personality that had kidnapped them. "How did you come to be made?" she asked.

"My master, Captain Michael, made me," Brian answered proudly. "He programmed me to speak, and he grew quite . . . he was quite fond of me."

Helena wondered if Brian's was the original interface that only a father could love. "What sort of man was he?" she asked, intrigued.

The pilot's monitor screen clicked off the image of the soupy atmosphere, and a still photograph replaced it. A broad-faced, dark-haired man looked impassively at the camera. The portrait clicked off, and another came on of the same man laughing; then it went and was replaced by the same man glowering sternly.

"That's him," confirmed Brian, "that's my father."

The picture show was interrupted as Koenig's voice came clearly through the speakers. "Koenig calling Swift. I have reached the mother ship. I'll have to go around to the blind side to get up to the airlocks."

"All right, Koenig," responded Brian. "Go ahead. But hurry."

"John? John?" questioned Helena in vain as the radio contact clicked dead.

"Easy, lady." Brian rolled back into the console. "We can't contact him now till he comes out."

Koenig had no trouble finding his way around the large mother ship, as all the corridors were plainly marked and he could remember something about the layout from his early training courses on Earth. He headed first for the Control Room, to check on the levels and stability of the fuel stores. He also wanted to see if there was a Captain's log in evidence that might tell him more about the fate of the mission.

As he made his way through the ship, he turned on the lights and discovered that the auxiliary power was functioning normally. The ship was sealed and pressurized, as well, so he slipped open his helmet plate.

The Control Room door swished hospitably open, and he stepped into the long, dimly lit room where one of man's ill-fated leaps to the stars had been directed on its course. Koenig located the control panel by the door and switched on the main, overhead lights. As he turned around he was almost knocked over by surprise.

"Hi, there, Commander," Tony said with a smile, lowering his laser.

Maya stood just behind him, grinning with relief.

"Tony! Maya!" Koenig shook his head.

Tony explained. "We landed ahead of you and came aboard to wait."

At last Koenig started to understand. He frowned. "Then you must have seen . . ."

"Yes," Maya said. "It was terrible. When we landed,

33

I ran a check on the atmosphere. In itself it's all right, but that mist is a complex and very violent poisonous gas . . . and it blankets the whole planet."

Tony waved his hands in the air with agitation. "And they went out there without their spacesuits. They must've been crazy." He gestured across the room and added, "They hadn't even sealed the ship. When we came in, we had to close the airlocks and completely reprocess the atmosphere."

Koenig looked down at the end of the room where Tony had motioned and saw a man slumped across the circular command desk. He walked back to it and looked down at the deskplate that read: "CAPTAIN V. MICHAEL."

Just enough of the man's face showed under his outflung arm for Koenig to tell that he, too, had the distorted features of a poisoned death agony. He had simply sat there at his post, and the deadly mist had come to him through the wide-flung doors of the ship. And outside, the crew calmly strolled to their terrible deaths. Koenig tried to reason why. Then he had a ghastly thought.

"Maya," he asked, "can you run a quick check on this ship's intelligence system?"

"Yes, sir." She stepped up to the Captain's console as Tony and Koenig moved the body out of the way and let it carefully down to the floor.

Maya activated the board and brought all the response circuits to glowing life. She clicked through to the room's master screen and waited for Koenig to give her a question to feed to the computer.

"See if it will give us the last entry in the mission's log," Koenig instructed.

Maya coded the request and looked up at the screen. The response was immediate . . . a languorously weaving sine wave.

"The same as on Moon Base!" said Tony.

Koenig felt his suspicions confirmed. "That Brian is madder than I thought."

Maya spoke her own reasoning out loud. "It blinded the computer and the sensors on its own mother ship.

34

That's why the crew didn't know about the toxic gas. It killed them all."

Koenig walked away slowly, considering the information, but also very aware that he must soon get back to the Swift. Helena's life was more at risk than he'd first thought.

Tony walked over to join him. "Why did it kidnap you?" he asked.

Koenig looked up gravely. "It wants me to transfer the fuel from this ship to the Swift."

Maya looked puzzled.

"It told us that it wants to live forever."

"So what do we do now?" asked Tony.

Koenig shrugged. "I'm going to get the fuel and take it back. We can't risk Helena's life."

"I don't suppose we can get her away from the Swift somehow and blow the little monster up?"

Koenig shook his head vigorously. "Wouldn't work," he explained. "He'll hold Helena until I get back with the fuel. And there's another reason . . . a very important one. That Swift has the only working computer in this part of the universe that's capable of replacing the memory store that's been blanked out at Moon Base. If we don't get that, we'll all die anyway."

Koenig moved quickly down the room to the door to the Captain's private office. According to routine procedure, the key to unlock the ship's fuel store would be inside. He stepped in with Tony and Maya right behind.

On one wall he spotted the small case with the set of Captain's keys hanging in neat rows behind the perspex. Captain Michael had left his office behind in a bit of a turmoil. Wiring diagrams and pieces of electrical equipment were scattered across the floor and on table tops everywhere.

Maya walked to the center of the room and looked carefully at a rectangular steel frame with plates bolted on two sides. Several printed circuit panels had already been fitted into place, the unconnected color-coded wires spraying outward like frozen party streamers.

"It looks like Captain Michael was working on something before he died," Maya observed.

"Well, that doesn't matter now," Tony said.

Koenig paused and looked at the half-completed device that Maya was inspecting and then glanced quickly at the circuit diagrams. "I'm not so sure," he disagreed thoughtfully. "I think it may be more meaningful than you might guess. Look, Tony, you go back to Eagle One and tell the pilot to stand by, but don't make any move till you hear from me. Maya and I will find the fuel store, unlock the core, and get it back to the Swift."

When Tony had hurried off, Maya looked at Koenig and asked, "What's the plan, Commander?"

"We're going to have to work on Brian's Brain. We'll have to break its mind."

Maya frowned.

"We've got to confuse it to the extent that it won't know what it's doing. I've seen that it can get very excited and irrational. We'll try to push it over the limit." Koenig winked. "Did you get a look a Captain Michael's face, Maya?"

"Yes," she said, recalling the features underneath the grimace of death and visualizing how they would have looked normally. "Yes, I did."

Helena waited fretfully in the pilot's compartment of the Swift, watching and listening anxiously for Koenig's return. Brian's casualness had worn pretty thin, as well.

"That Koenig's taking his own damn sweet time!" he complained.

Helena realized that Koenig might be working out a plan and might be needing extra minutes. It was also possible that something had happened to him, but she knew she could not do any good worrying about that. So instead she tried to pacify Brian.

"I don't think so," she said. "He has to find the fuel store, unlock the core, and find a way to bring it back."

Brian wasn't very much appeased. "Lady, you don't know what this means to me. Is that guy reliable?"

"He's reliable," she answered with certainty.

The Brain's tri-lens suddenly clicked around to a stronger magnification. "There he is!" he yelled joyfully.

Helena had to wait another few seconds before she made out the vague details of Koenig's suit coming through the clouds. In his arms he cradled a large metal cylinder.

"John! John!" she shouted into the microphone.

This time he heard her, and his voice came crackling back. "Koenig to Swift. I am returning with the mother ship's fuel store."

The Brain was flashing lights almost enough to blow a fuse. "Have you got it all, Koenig? Have you got it all?" The voice was demanding. "Koenig, answer me!"

Refusing to be intimidated, Koenig responded matter-of-factly, "Koenig to Swift. Are you ready to receive me?"

"Yessss!" Brian wailed deliriously.

When Koenig at last climbed back into the Swift's passenger compartment and came through the airlock, Helena was waiting to rush up and hug him. Brian scooted back and forth anxiously as she helped him take the spacesuit off.

The cylinder sat at the back of the module, still attached to the hoist cable that Brian had lowered down to bring it up.

"Come on, Koenig! Come on!" niggled Brian.

"Give him time," Helena said sternly.

As she turned back to help unfasten the suit, she looked into Koenig's eyes and tried to decipher the message that was there. Obviously something had been planned, a fact that was confirmed by the significant way that Koenig leaned down and gave her two perfunctory kisses on the lips. She couldn't guess what he was scheming, but she kept herself alert and ready to respond to his lead.

"Cut it out, folks!" Brian had no time for demonstrations of affection. "Koenig, get that fuel!"

"Take it easy," he replied. "I haven't got the suit off yet."

Helena smoothed back the dark hair from his forehead. It was slightly damp from the work of carrying the cylinder and from tension.

"How was it?" she asked.

"Not too bad." Then with an edge in his voice he spoke directly to Brian. "Your crew is out there, scattered all over the place. Very dead."

"So they're dead, so what!" he snapped back.

Koenig had shed the spacesuit but he didn't move toward the fuel, simply stood facing Brian with a scowl of accusation. "I found Captain Michael in the Control Room. He was sitting dead at his desk . . . but then you must know that already."

The Brain had stopped still from its ceaseless rolling back and forth. The panel lights pulsed with anxious currents, and the metal of the cabinet almost visibly shuddered. "My father?" he asked.

Koenig nodded sternly.

"Ahhh . . ." Brian wheeled around and headed for the back of the passenger section. "Get this fuel loaded, Koenig!"

A panel at the top of the after part of the module slid open. From behind it a large clear tube telescoped down toward the metal cannister. Koenig moved around Brian and walked slowly back.

The cylinder with its thick protective layer was very heavy, and Koenig grunted as he heaved it off the floor. He carried it along and set it down just under the extended tube.

"Up!" Brian ordered. "Lift it up, Koenig!"

"Wait a minute, Brian." Koenig rubbed his fingers where the edge of the cannister had cut into them. "Which end goes in first?" "Which end is up?"

Brian seemed stumped. "What? What does it say?"

Koenig looked at the blank sides and shook his head.

Suddenly Brian's lights rippled crossly. "Those fuel cores are symmetrical! Any end is up. Stop fooling, Koenig!"

Grinning wryly, Koenig bent down and lifted the cylinder up to the tube. As it slipped in, there was a whoosh and it shot up out of sight. The tube quickly withdrew, and the panel closed behind it.

"Zowie! Powie!" celebrated Brian, rolling gaily and blinking like a casino sign. "Zappity-rappity-bap. Oh, boppity-hoppity-poy! Boy, oh boy, do I feel good! Oh waw-waw-waw! Oh, boy, far out! WA-OW! That fuel is too much, folks. I mean it's outta sight! Just about blown my marvellous old mind straight into nirvana." He let loose a metallic harsh-sounding laugh, rather like the sound of a saucepan falling down a stone flight of stairs. "This is the happiest day of my life. I'm free! Can you dig that? I'm free to roam this universe . . . free to live forever." He whirled around and charged full tilt for the pilot's cabin, shouting, "Stand by for takeoff!"

Koenig and Helena just had time to throw themselves into a seat before the rockets roared and the Swift lifted up. As soon as the takeoff force receded, Koenig unzipped a pocket on his jacket and took out a small brown mouse.

Helena turned to watch what he was doing, and her eyes widened in surprise. Then she understood, and quickly figured that Koenig must have met Maya when he went on board the mother ship. She felt a lifting surge of hope to know they now had the Psychon's transformation talents to aid them.

Koenig gently placed the mouse on the floor, and it scampered up to the dooorway of the pilot section where Brian sat still, monitoring the flight information from the ship's controls. The mouse paused, then ran along the length of the Brain's trailing ground-contact antennae.

"What's happening?" screeched Brian, jerking forward. "What's that? What's that?" The tri-lens spun around trying to see what was happening.

"It's a mouse," said Helena.

"Ahh! Ahh!" Brian whined. "Get rid of it, it's biting my antennae!"

As Brian backed into the module and turned completely to face his attacker, the mouse began to disappear, becoming a flickering ripple of light and energy. The molecular disturbance flared brightly and Maya suddenly appeared, standing in the passageway between the seats.

"Where the heck did you come from?" demanded Brian.

"Planet D," she told him.

"But you were a mouse! There are no mice on Planet D! There's nothing there at all! The gas ... the ..." Brian stuttered to a confused halt.

"I came from Planet D," repeated Maya. "I have a message for you."

"Message? Whattya mean, message?"

Maya smiled wickedly. "It's a message from Captain Michael."

The Brain jerked back, spinning its wheels in fright. "Huh? He's ... he's DEAD! What message?"

"Revenge." Maya's smile widened to let light glint off the points of her teeth.

Brian wailed and rolled rapidly into the pilot section, the door crashing closed behind him. The Swift's lights began to blink rapidly off and on as an alert siren began to wail and an alarm bell clanged violently. Maya, Koenig, and Helena threw their hands over their ears, grimacing from the frenzied decibels of The Brain's panic.

CHAPTER FOUR

They were trapped in the passenger section for nearly five minutes while the emergency signals battered their eardrums. Koenig wondered how badly The Brain was affected and whether or not he might even crash the ship.

When it finally stopped, there was a long silence, almost as if Brian had actually shorted all his circuits. Koenig waited expectantly, knowing that he would have to force the door and get control of the Swift if Brian really had become disfunctional. He wanted to be sure, and even hushed Helena when she started to speak, in case Brian was all right and secretly observing them. Minutes ticked by.

They all twitched with fear when the door did slide open and Brian rattled slowly out again. He confronted them with a slow pan of the tri-lens, and the amber light snapped off and on with anger.

"You don't have no message from Captain Michael!" it said to Maya. "I remember you now from Moon Base. You're a friend of Koenig and the Doctor. That was a pretty neat trick, mouse woman, but you're only a mortal. What chance do you think you stand against me?" The tri-lens flicked back and forth in disapproval. "I am in complete control of this spaceship and everything aboard it. You're a fool to come in here, because ... I'm going to blow the whole damn bunch of you into space. Whaddya think about that, huh?"

Koenig took a step forward. "Just tell us one thing, Brian. Why did you kill your creator?"

The tri-lens swung away from Koenig, refusing to take in the accusing eyes. "I did not kill my creator." The voice started to whimper.

"He was sitting at his command desk, dead. And *you* killed him."

"I did not kill him!" the Tri-lens stared resolutely the other way. "I don't know how he died."

Koenig stepped around into Brian's field of view. "He is dead because you blinded his computer. He didn't know the gas was poisonous, so his crew went outside and died in it ... and the airlock wasn't sealed so the gas came into the ship and killed him, too."

Maya took the cue, saying incredulously, "You mean he murdered the man who made him?"

"His own father?" chipped in Helena. "But why?"

The Brain urgently flashed his lights in discomfort.

"We know why you killed him, Brian," Koenig said loudly. "He was working on an improved model of you. You were going to be made obsolete. You were going to be scrapped."

"No! No! That isn't true! He wasn't!"

Koenig continued relentlessly. "We saw it. Your days were numbered, and so you decided to kill them all off by keeping them from knowing about the gas. You blinded the mother ship to keep a new Brain from being made to take your place."

The display of lights went berserk again, popping on and off like fireworks. He didn't seem to have full control over his mobility, and he bumped into the wall as he rolled from side to side.

"Aaaargh," he groaned in pain, amber light fluttering against the glass like a trapped bird. "Aaaargh. My father *was not* working on a better Brain! There can't *be* a better Brain!"

Helena said soothingly, "Calm down, Brian. You're getting overexcited."

"Yes. Yes. I shouldn't become excited."

Maya leaned over to look very closely in the tri-lens. "I think you need maintenance."

Koenig, too, stepped close and said, "We'll make a bargain with you, Brian. We'll give you maintenance—give you the check-over you need—and then you let us go unharmed."

There was a moment of expectant silence. Not even the rumble of the rockets could be heard inside the Swift. Brian quieted his lights down to a dull glow as he considered the proposition.

The amber gushed brightly, and he rolled away from them. "Oh, no, you don't! I'm going to blow you all out into space!"

"But who will repair you then?" argued Koenig. "You must have maintenance. Ask the Doctor if you don't believe me."

Helena nodded. "You must have maintenance, Brian."

Maya indicated her assent as well, and they all closed in on the gradually retreating box again. The viewing lens swept back and forth as he tried to test the information they were feeding him by assembling it into a new program.

"I'll maintain you!" offered Koenig.

"*I'll* maintain you!" said Maya.

Helena shouted just as loudly. "No. *I'll* maintain you!"

"You'll have to decide, Brian. Choose between us."

Brian made a tentative lunge forward, as if to drive them back. "What is this?" he wailed. "What is this game? You all know what each other one is up to. How do you do that?"

"You control other computers with your brainwaves," explained Helena. "We can do that, too. It's called being in tune with somebody."

"Instinct," added Koenig. "Now come on, Brian. Make your mind up. Which of us is it to be?"

He look suspiciously from face to face. "How do I know which of you is the best engineer?"

"Me!"

"Me!"

"Me!"

The lens snapped back and forth.

"Take me!"

"Take me!"

Brian just wanted the problem to stop. "All right, you." It looked at Koenig.

"No, me!"

"Me!"

As the lens swung frantically around once again to follow the hectoring voices it saw the face of its beloved and dead creator ... Captain Michael. For a moment the information read like a leakage from the memory track, a random image echo that should clear instantly. But it didn't, and as The Brain ran a test on his own video input, he realized that the optical impression was actual. Captain Michael was there!

"WHEEP WHEEP WHEEP!" Brian gave a horrified scream and backed up as fast as he could, crashing straight into the wall. The impact shattered some of the glasses on his monitor lights and loosed enough sparks

43

inside his circuits to blow out a small cloud of blue smoke.

Koenig felt a sideways pull that told him the Swift was now out of control, obviously not being navigated any more by some of Brian's autonomic functions. He just hoped that they could beat him into submission before something more serious happened to the craft.

Maya, transferred into the image of Capain Michael, adamantly confronted Brian. His lights were all pulsing in unison, beating like a labored heart.

"What did you do to me?" asked Captain Michael.

"It was a mistake! It was, it was . . a mis—mistake."

"You killed me. You horrible machine. You murderer!"

Brian's lens jerked about in terror, looking for a route of escape. "No! No!" he protested.

"I conceived you," the Captain persisted. "I made you. I am wiser and greater than you. And you killed me." The tenor of the voice became cuttingly sarcastic. "No wonder I decided to make a better Brain than you. You were so mean and small . . . so pathetic!"

Brian swerved past Captain Michael and backed toward the airlocks. The only sound it made then was a scratching whine of its vocal reproduction tape cartridge spinning out of control. The Captain turned and stalked remorsefully forward, a pointing finger thrust forward like a divine gesture of banishment.

Gibbering and sobbing, Brian rolled right back into the waiting airlock. As soon as he was over the threshold, Koenig flung himself forward and slapped the button to close the clear internal panel. It slipped quickly across, and Koenig thumbed the switch for the external door. With a whoosh Brian popped neatly out into space and Koenig closed the door hurriedly behind him.

Koenig didn't wait to watch Maya transform back into her own appearance. He reckoned that congratulations could wait until they were sure they were justified.

Running the best he could against the unbalancing spin of the Swift, he made for the flight deck. He jumped into the pilot's seat and tested the controls for response. When he had an affirmative indication, he corrected the spin of the craft and got it coasting forward on a slow, level course.

Next he turned on the exterior cameras and looked around for any sign of Brian. Remarkably, he was still with them, trailing along next to the airlock with his antennae caught in the door. He gave no signs of life; all his lights were extinguished.

"Swift to Eagle One," Koenig barked anxiously into the radio. "Swift to Eagle One. Are you with us?"

Straight away the reply came back, and the faces of both Tony and the Eagle One pilot crowded onto the video screen. "John!" yelled Tony. "Are you all right?"

"We're all fine," Koenig confirmed. "Where are you?"

"Not far away, Commander," the pilot advised. "We've been keeping you in view without getting too close."

"Fine. Fine. Well, you can come alongside now and take us aboard. Swift out."

Helena joined him in the cabin and patted his shoulder. "What now, John?"

"Our next problem is to locate the memory core of The Brain's computer . . . then hope it isn't damaged and that we can transfer it back to Moon Base."

"Well, I suppose this is where you need a computer expert?" Maya glided beautifully into the compartment.

Koenig nodded his agreement. "That's right. And by the way, that was an excellent job you did there. Thanks very much."

Maya nodded modestly. "There's just one thing that worries me."

"What's that?" asked Koenig.

Maya pointed down to the screen that was still receiving the picture of The Brain trailing out from the airlock. "That's a hazard. With his antennae caught in the door like that, the seal isn't secure, and we could be risking a depressurization."

Koenig had already turned around and was looking along the front of the computer cabinet for a likely panel to conceal the memory store. "That's no problem," he said casually, "why don't we just cut it?"

The feeble, static-fevered voice that came through the

45

main speakers startled them all. "Because . . ." said Brian, "because, if you cut my antennae . . ." they could barely see that the lights on his box were very faintly lit, "my memory core will be wiped clean. Moon Base will be blind forever."

Koenig lunged down to growl into the microphone, "Is that the truth, Brian? Or is it just another damn lie?"

The Brain tried desperately to reassert his power. "If you don't get me back in, *right now*, I'll wipe it clean anyway."

Koenig decided to call his bluff. "I'll take a chance on that." Over his shoulder he commanded Maya, "Cut his antennae!"

Brian screeched, "NO NO NO! Don't cut my antennae. Please don't cut my antennae!"

Very firmly Koenig said, "All right, Brian. We'll let you live . . . IF you hand over your memory core to us, undamaged."

They could have sworn that The Brain was crying, so sob-like were its noises. "Yes. Yes, take my memory. Take it all." A diagram of the computer circuits flashed on a monitor. Maya studied it carefully, noting the memory storage and how to retrieve it. "All I wanted was to live," Brian moaned on. "Just to live."

Koenig couldn't feel confident that Brian the Brain had really been defeated until they were all back in the Control Center at Alpha and the Swift's memory had been fully and safely programmed into the Moon Base computer.

Maya looked up from her familiar place at the monitor and smiled across to him. "Memory programming complete, sir. All tests affirmative."

Koenig glanced at Yasko and Tony, who both nodded agreement. Finally he let himself take a deep breath and relax in his chair. All around the Command Center the full complement of staff felt themselves relax with him and got down to the urgent business of getting the Moon Base back to normal operation.

"Tony," Koenig said, "give me a status check on all

vital systems and all departments. Start with the most urgent data." .

"Let's start where we left off, then . . ." Tony looked over at Maya, unable to hide his grin of gladness that she was back where he could keep an eye on her. "Could we have a horizon check, Maya? Let's find out where we're going."

Maya fed the information through to the big screen so all the personnel could see it. The letters shone out brightly as they flashed up:

HORIZON STABLE—DIRECTION UNCHANGED

Helena shook her head. "So it was just another lie by The Brain. He had our computer misleading us before we even knew he was there. The Moon is still on course."

Koenig nodded and turned to Tony for the next report. "The tiranium stocks are very depleted, Commander," he said, looking at the print-out. "Because of insufficient computer information during the blackout, too much was used too quickly."

"How bad is it?"

Tony checked the computer assessment. "Unless we build up the stocks, the situation will approach critical in about a month's time."

Koenig smacked his hand down hard on the arm of his chair. Tiranium was the one rare element that the entire power system of Alpha was set up to use. Without it the artificial environment would begin to fail and even the computer functions would quickly collapse. The restored memory bank would do them no good then.

Helena, too, was dismayed at the news, since tiranium was essential to many of the medical treatments for difficult surgical operations, such as parts replacement.

"That doesn't sound very promising," said Koenig. "Get me full details right away. It looks like we've got quite a lot to thank Brian the Brain for."

Maya looked up. "What do you intend to do about The Brain, sir?"

"I don't know. Let's have a look at it."

Up on the big screen a telescopic picture of the Swift flashed. It drifted silently through the blackness, its engines shut off. They could just see the outline of the dangling box that was Brian the Brain. Maya touched some more buttons and connected with the Swift's own system. The picture changed to a close-up of Brian, relayed through the Swift's external cameras.

"It doesn't look very threatening now," said Helena. "We've blinded it and taken its memory."

"Don't forget," said Tony, "that when it was operational, it killed a lot of people . . . and it wanted to kill you, too."

Maya sighed. "Strangely, it did feel some form of guilt, at least about Captain Michael's death."

Helena nodded, then added, "It cried . . . or something like it."

Koenig looked questioningly at Tony, waiting for his suggestion. The Italian grimaced and flung up his hands. "So all right," he conceded, "we could re-install its memory core now that we've copied it. But just think how dangerous he would be then. He could come after us and get his revenge by knocking out our computer again."

Koenig laid a finger thoughtfully against his lips and wondered what was the best thing to do. He was reluctant to condemn a consciousness, even an electronic one, to float for eternity . . . unseeing and mindless. "What if we erase the memory core before we take it back. Then The Brain can start learning from scratch . . . with no guilt or ambitions of immortality to screw him up. It'll take a few hundred years for him to educate himself, but that's not much out of a billion."

Tony nodded agreement and connected himself to the pilots' station. "Command Center to Pilots," he said. "Stand by Eagle One for takeoff. You will be returning computer memory core to the Swift."

Koenig pushed himself out of the chair and decided that a cup of tasteless synthetic coffee would be about the best thing he could ever ask for right then. He walked over to where Helena was talking to Maya.

"Helena," he asked with a tired smile, "do we have any off-duty time that coincides about now?"

"From the sound of the state we're in now, I don't think there's going to be any off-duty time for a month or so." She smiled back at him with regret.

"That's too bad. I was looking forward to a chance of discussing that love test with you."

Maya looked up questioningly. "What test was that, sir?"

Koening kept his eyes on Helena's, seeing the twinkle of amusement there. "Oh, it was a test devised by The Brain."

Helena laughed lightly. "We failed it," she said.

CHAPTER FIVE

Alan Carter knew that he shouldn't really be in the tunnels, but he was absolutely fed up with sitting on his backside in the pilot's day room with nothing to do but play cards. Since the tiranium shortage became known, the Eagles had been used as sparingly as possible, as even the meager amounts of the precious element they required couldn't be lightly spared.

In any case, he justified his journey beneath the surface as just adding another good pair of eyes to the frantic search to uncover a tiranium deposit. He was an old friend of Andy Johnson, the red-haired young mineralogist who was driving the moonbuggy, so he had little difficulty persuading him to let him come along. The geological survey had only just broken through into a new system of natural caverns the day before, and throughout the night oxygen had been pumped into them so that the survey teams could go in and explore.

Alan was enjoying the ride, watching the silent darkness of the tunnel roll back before the powerful moonbuggy floodlights. It was a damn sight more interesting than another bloody game of rummy!

"Roll on, cobber!" he shouted jovially. "Roll on, and let's you and me find us a pot of gold down here. Fair dinkum that would be!"

Andy laughed at his boyish exuberance. "A handful of tiranium pebbles, old buddy, would be worth a hundred tons of gold to us right now. And I think we get to the walking part of this trip about now."

The moonbuggy jerked to a stop, and they looked ahead where the lights showed the tunnel narrowing to a slim passageway.

"That looks interesting," commented Carter.

"Well, let's go see, then." Andy climbed out and opened the equipment hatch. "Grab that radiant lamp and I'll bring the sonarscope."

"You think this place looks promising, then?"

Andy nodded enthusiastically. "You see that fault line there? Well, it's an indication that the stresses which affected this particular line of the subvolcanic strata—"

"Hold on, mate," Carter protested, "all I asked was if it looked promising. How come any time I ask you what the time is, you always put me through a university course on how a watch is made?"

"Huh?" Andy chuckled and returned the jibe. "I always wondered the same thing about you and your astronaut training. Like when I ask you what that little black button on the control panel of your Eagle is . . . and I get a whole chapter of the flight manual recited to me."

Alan joined in Andy's laughter and hefted out the lamp. He led the way into the crevice, just comfortably wide enough to walk through. On the other side he came into a large natural cavern and clicked the lamp on. He set it on the ground, and its glow increased until it filled the chamber.

"Well, well, well . . ." said Andy and began to assemble his equipment.

Alan helped him spread out the solid tripod legs and set the sonar tube on the swivel mounting. Johnson checked the power pack and turned it on.

"All right," he said, "stand by to scan."

A sharp, highly stabilized light beam sliced out of the tube and Andy directed it onto the cavern wall. Alan stood to one side, checking the dial which showed the electromagnetic field reading of minerals and ores. Andy kept his fingers poised over the cutting wave control ready to excavate and uncover deeper layers of the soft Moon soil.

First they tried the left wall, then the right wall, and finally the one right in front of them. On the third pass across that, about five feet from the cave floor, there was a sharp whine from the sonar sensor.

"I've got a reading," confirmed Alan.

Andy moved the beam horizontally, then vertically to get a coordinated point for the strongest signal. When he found it he switched on the probe, detecting only by the slight shudder through his arms that the sonic waves were pounding against the friable rock. After a moment of concentrated drilling there was a sharp bell sound from the sensor, and Alan saw the dial needle make a sharp leap.

"That's it!" he yelled.

Andy switched off the probe and walked over to the small, neat perforation in the wall, motes of pulverized dust still swirling around. He selected a long narrow pick from his belt and slid it into the hole, digging gently. As he pulled it out, a small blue chip of stone came with it, falling into his hand.

"Well, what do you know?" he said. "There really is tiranium in them thar hills!"

Andy passed the stone over to Alan to look at and to store in the sample bag and got ready to scan another section of the wall. He had hardly turned the machine on when it suddenly squealed loudly. This time the sound didn't die away, but kept up its intensity as he swung the beam across.

"Hey!" he said excitedly. "This is a big one!"

He maneuvered the beam back and forth until he had determined the long straight edge of what the machine was detecting behind the rock. "We might have us a whole seam of tiranium here!" he shouted, turning the cutting wave up to full power.

The cave wall began to vibrate steadily under the force, and slowly the face of it began to peel away in a crumbling of pebbles and dust. It had penetrated about three feet when the middle of the window-sized hole cleared to show a gleam of silvery metal. Andy abruptly cut the machine off.

"Hey! That's no tiranium deposit!" he said in surprise.

Alan shook his head in bafflement. There was not enough revealed to tell what it was. Andy switched on again and began clearing the rock to either side. Eventually it was shaped into a large doorway, about seven feet high by five feet wide. Set back in it was something like a large cabinet, framed in shining metal but mostly made of a transparent material, coated with dust.

Alan moved closer and stared hard. "There's something inside," he announced.

Andy shut off the machine and moved the lamp closer so it would throw more light directly into the cavity. More dust slid away from the front of the box, and Alan swallowed hard.

"There's *somebody* inside!" he moved a step closer. "It looks like a man and a young boy . . . like a couple of corpses."

Andy was feeling very puzzled. "But that rock hasn't been disturbed for millions of years!"

Alan nodded. "Yeah, I know, but . . ." Suddenly his head jerked up. "Hold it!"

"What is it?"

"I thought . . . just for a moment . . ." Before he said what it was he thought he saw, he moved right up to the front window panel, looking carefully at the hazy outline of the man's body inside. There was still too much dust

52

to see clearly, so he raised his hand and wiped away the glass just over the face.

As his hand touched the glass, it became bathed in a green, blinding light. Carter screamed in agony, his hand sealed against the glass is if by high voltage. He felt himself blacking out, then he began to fall, feeling nothing as he crashed to the ground.

"Alan! Alan!" Andy shouted as he rushed up and knelt down. He checked quickly to see if Carter was still breathing, which he was, but in sharp agonized gasps.

Glancing up at the glass where Alan's hand had been trapped, he could clearly see through the cleared glass. Underneath was a stark, angular face ... and the deep, large eyes were coldly looking right at him.

In terror he scrambled to where he had dropped his Comlock.

The Alpha Emergency Team went about their work with smooth efficiency. One of the technicians had moved the sonarscope right up close to the mysterious cabinet and was very carefully clearing the rock away from either side under the guidance of Tony Verdeschi. He and the rest of the team were taking every caution not to get too close or to touch the box's sides.

Farther back in the cavern, Alan had been moved on a stretcher and Helena and Doctor Ben Vincent were checking him over carefully. She passed a bioscan over his chest and smiled to see that he was recovering nicely.

Doctor Vincent saw that his help wouldn't be needed and walked off to prepare the equipment to see if any readings could be taken off the beings in the cabinet. With added illumination and the glass front air-blasted, it could now be clearly seen that two people were inside, a man and a boy of about fourteen years. They were standing stiff and straight as statues, eyes firmly closed.

Alan Carter's eyes, however, began to flicker open, and he made out the details of Helena's face as his vision adjusted to the light. She smiled and laid a pressure gun against his arm to inject a mild analgesic.

53

"As our Search and Rescue Medical Team would say after they find one of our crashed astronauts who has been lying unconscious on a strange planet for two days with a broken arm, contusions, three cracked ribs, and a fractured leg . . . Hey, are you all right?"

Since the pain-killer hadn't quite started to take effect, Alan groaned as he sat up. "I feel like I've been slugged by a bleedin' kangaroo."

"Only stunned a little is my medical diagnosis," grinned Helena.

Alan rubbed the back of his neck. "Easy for you to say. You don't have my head."

Tony and Andy walked over to join them as Alan got to his feet. Alan nodded to them both that he was quickly recovering from his shock. Not altogether seriously, Tony chided Alan for coming into the tunnels in the first place.

"I only wanted a little excitement," Alan protested, "and I guess I found it."

Tony laughed. "Anybody got any theories about that thing yet?"

Helena and Andy both shook their heads. Alan frowned, then suggested, "Maybe it's some kind of cryogenic, suspended-animation setup."

"Let's see," said Helena as she led the way over to where Doctor Vincent was monitoring the medical sensors trained on the cabinet. The round face of the scope showed two straight and steady lines of light. She pressed a button and the lines disappeared and were replaced by the temperature reading of the cabinet's interior. It read "Temp. 4°C."

"Hmm. It's cool in there, but well above the cryogenic temperature range."

Helena tried another button and the steady, unbroken lines returned. Doctor Vincent shrugged. "That's it," he said. "No sign of life at any level. No brain activity . . . no heartbeat . . . no respiration."

"Some form of burial, then?" proposed Tony.

Helena frowned. "A bit elaborate for a tomb, don't you think? Surrounded by a strong force field. Who are they being protected from?"

"Us?"

Andy had been debating with himself about whether to interrupt. Suddenly he felt he couldn't keep his thoughts to himself any longer. "I've got news for you. That's no tomb." They all looked at him. "You don't bury people until they're dead, and the big guy in there, he's alive."

"Our sensor doesn't agree with you, Andy," said Helena.

Andy was adamant, remembering with a shudder the sight of those watching eyes. "Your sensor didn't see what I saw. Just after Alan fell, I looked up and saw him staring at me."

Helena turned to Alan. "Did *you* see anything like that?"

"Wait a minute," Andy cut in, "you think I flipped out or something?"

"You were under a strain," explained Helena. "You thought Alan had been killed. In moments of stress the mind can play strange tricks."

Andy wheeled about in irritation and marched across to the front of the cabinet. They all followed him, looking up as he did at the lifeless forms.

"I *saw* him!" Andy almost shouted. "His eyes were wide open!"

Tony looked toward the top of the cabinet and his eyes were attracted to a kind of design on the metal frame. He nudged Helena and pointed to it. From a globe-like base it curved upward, flame-like, to a pointed top.

"What do you suppose that means?" she asked.

Alan looked up too. "I bet it means that whoever touches this box gets clobbered."

Andy didn't think the idea was very funny. "From the look in that guy's eyes, it should mean that whoever touches that box gets killed. There was murder in—"

"Helena!" Doctor Vincent shouted over from the medical monitor.

They all turned, caught by the note of urgency in his voice.

"Just then . . . I picked up a heartbeat," he explained.

Helena glanced again at the cabinet, but the figures inside had not changed. Tony suddenly sensed that Andy hadn't been mistaken, that he *had* seen the man's eyes open.

"But only one heartbeat," he said wonderingly, "in all the time we've been here."

Helena had another thought. "Check the volume of air in the lungs . . . see if it has changed at all since you started monitoring."

The question clicked through the monitor and the reply flashed back on the scope screen for Doctor Vincent to read off to them. "Increase of 2.5 millimeters in just over seven minutes."

"He's breathing," gasped Helena, wondering at the slowness.

The cabinet captured their attention with new interest. The most important question had been resolved, and the mystery had deepened.

"How do we get them out?" asked Helena.

Tony bent down and picked up a small chip of rock from the ground. He aimed and flicked it at the cabinet with his thumb, and there was a flash of green and a loud snap as the force field shattered it.

"Very carefully," he replied.

The technician who was operating the sonarscope had nearly cleared away all the rock along one side, so that the depth of the box could be seen. A large chunk of Moonrock tumbled down and revealed that a small black box was fixed to the cabinet near the back.

"Mister Verdeschi!" the technician shouted. "Look at this."

Tony crowded past him into the opening and looked at the small rectangle which protruded about an inch from the side. On its front were a series of dials and buttons labelled in a code that meant absolutely nothing to him.

Alan and Helena moved in beside him after the excited technician had pulled the sonarscope back out of the way. In his own curiosity to see what was happening he tilted the scope tube so that it pointed upwards to the cave roof, but forgot to turn it off.

"It must be the power source," said Tony.

Alan nodded. "And the control panel. Do you think you can operate it?"

Tony picked up another rock chip and tossed it at the box. It hit the front and bounced off undamaged. "Well, I can touch it, anyway," said Tony, "but the problem is figuring out which button does what."

"First we need to know which one turns off the force field," Helena observed. "If only Maya were here, she'd figure it out in a second. Maybe we should wait and ask her to come down—"

Suddenly from overhead there came an ominous cracking sound and a small shower of pebbles trickled down on them. They all looked up and saw a deep crack spreading rapidly along the cavern's ceiling.

"Blimey!" yelled Alan. "The scope cutter is still on!"

The fissures of the main crack began to race away, spreading out like lightning. There was a frightful groan as the supporting dynamics of the vaulted ceiling began to fail. A giant slab of rock just above them edged downward with a creak.

Alan turned the scope off, but the splitting of the ceiling went on regardless. Tony waved the rest of the crew back toward the gap that led into the tunnel. Green sparks began to fly as the hail of stones popped against the force field.

"Back!" ordered Tony. "Everybody back!"

Helena resisted his insistent pulling. "Tony, we can't just leave them!"

"Get away, Helena!"

"But they're alive!" she still resisted. "We can't let them die!"

Tony hesitated, then dashed into the space beside the box. He looked desperately at the control panel's face, wondering which button would stop the force field and what might happen if he chose the wrong one. More and more stone was falling, larger pieces which were disintegrating with louder explosions.

One of the buttons was colored red and seemed somehow more likely than any of the others. Tony gritted his teeth and pressed it down. Suddenly the rocks stopped exploding and began to bounce off the cabinet's glass with clicks and thuds. He had made the right choice, but he knew they still had the problem of getting the thing open.

He was preparing to try another button when a great jagged piece of the main roof slab broke off and plummeted down. With no force field to deflect it, the boulder crashed into the front plate at an angle and the glass shattered with a dull thump of released pressure. The older man inside toppled forward and rolled over just in front of Helena.

Tony jumped over to help her and Alan drag the man back toward the safer part of the cavern. Heavy rocks were crashing all around them as the slab above shifted once more.

"The boy!" Alan shouted abruptly, spinning around.

Tony tried to grab his arm as he sprinted back through the haze of dust toward the cabinet. "It'll go any second!" he shouted after him.

The boy was slumped down inside, his legs covered by a pile of small rocks and shattered glass. Alan tugged him out of it and lifted him easily in his arms. As he turned to run back, another big chunk fell and bounced onto his foot, pinning it against the cabinet. Looking up, he saw the slab slipping toward its last support and with one enormous effort yanked his foot free and dashed for the back of the cave.

The ceiling suddenly gave way with a roar like cannons, the slab smashing straight onto the cabinet and bringing after it tons and tons of rock. The jolt of impact made the cave floor bounce and Alan tripped to the ground, sheltering the boy's body from flying debris.

As the rumbles died away and the dust began to settle, he looked up to see that everyone was safe. He let the boy down easily and brushed the dirt off his face as Tony knelt down next to him.

"You were really pushing your luck that time," he said.

Alan looked at him. "He's just a kid. I couldn't leave him there."

Helena was already working deftly on the man, trying to discern if he had any injuries. Doctor Vincent joined her with the bioscan and held it above the man's chest.

"Heartbeat!" he announced tersely. He turned the dial, and added, "And there's a brain pulse! It's increasing."

Soon the man's mouth began to move. He didn't really have any lips, but a colorless, severe line that weakly opened. In a strained, rumbling voice, he said, "Etrec! Etrec!"

"He must mean the boy," said Doctor Vincent.

Helena gestured. "Take the monitor over to him."

As Vincent took the equipment over, Helena tried to comfort the man. "Take it easy," she said soothingly. "You'll be all right."

The man's mouth continued to form the same word, over and over again. Then his hand moved, instinctively edging toward where the boy was lying. Helena touched his chest as a sign to be still and moved over to join the group around the boy.

Doctor Vincent looked up from the monitor. "I got a heartbeat," he announced.

Helena ordered, "Put him on pure oxygen."

Reaching behind him, Doctor Vincent lifted the breathing mask around and fitted it over the boy's face.

"Now pump the chest," Helena advised.

While Vincent pressed regularly down on the small ribcage to stimulate breathing, Helena ran a quick check for any other injuries. She was relieved that he seemed all right and even more pleased that a brain pulse and the heartbeat rate were starting to pick up for him, too.

As they gathered around, watching anxiously to see whether the lad would recover, the body of the man behind them began to stir. His eyes snapped open, and he turned his head carefully to see where he was.

The first thing he could clearly make out was the backs of the people leaning over Etrec. His expression twisted slowly into a grimace of hatred, and a light began to shine in the skin of his forehead. The glow became stronger and more horrific, as if the tortured metal of a furnace-blasted branding iron were trapped inside the flesh. It formed the distinctive, flame-like symbol that had been embossed over the top of the cabinet.

On the ground nearby his eyes caught sight of a gleaming long miner's pick which had been dropped by one of the survey team. Agonizingly he reached out for it, his fingers clawing in desperation. The strain became too much, and abruptly he sighed and fell back, unconscious.

Doctor Vincent smiled around the circle of anxious faces. "Brain and heart picking up strongly," he reported.

"Levels?" asked Helena.

"Brain seven seven three and rising. Heart . . . forty-four, forty-five, forty-six. Increasing steadily."

Alan looked questioningly at Helena. "Is he safe?"

She nodded. "As safe as we all are." She stood up with a yawn to get the tension out of her face muscles. Looking over at the older man, she could see he was still resting the way she had left him. Her eyes felt strained by all the dust still hanging around so she didn't feel perturbed by the slight red glow that seemed to hover over his forehead and then fade away. It was so simply an optical illusion that she didn't give it a second thought.

CHAPTER SIX

The two aliens lay side by side in the Medical Center, resting quietly. In sleep their faces had the death-like blankness that they had worn inside the cabinet. But now Helena had only to check the life systems monitor to be sure they were safely alive. In fact, she could clearly see the deep, rhythmic rise and fall of their chests.

Tiredly she rubbed her eyes, wishing uselessly that John had not been called away to the emergency in the

Blue Quadrant mining survey. She didn't know what communications problems there might be when the two revived, and she would feel more confident if he were there to help ... or if Maya were, but she, too, had gone on the mission. Well, she would just have to make them as comfortable, and as welcome, as possible.

She switched on the recorder on her desk to make her daily report. "Moon Base Alpha Medical Section. Doctor Helena Russell recording. Special Incident Report. Excavation Discovery Supplementary ... Medical. Both subjects resting quietly, cardiac stimuli no longer necessary." She paused as Doctor Vincent came over to hand her some further readings from the tests they were running. She glanced through them and continued, "Monitoring of all physical functions is being maintained. Preliminary analysis indicates a cell structure and metabolism ninety-one point seven percent of human norm. Minor differences in blood chemistry and brain pattern. Further investigations being carried out."

Helena turned off the recorder and went around to join Doctor Vincent and one of the orderlies who was assisting him.

"How well are they sleeping?" she asked.

The orderly looked at the EEG needles scratching their peaks and valleys on the recording graph. "They're sleeping very deeply."

"Natural or sedated?"

"Sedated," said Doctor Vincent. "They're still on Somnol."

"Take them off it," Helena instructed, and the orderly moved around and pulled off the osmosis patch on each alien's forearm.

Doctor Vincent nodded. "All readings stable. Shall we get on with programming the computer for detailed functional analysis?"

Helena wished she could take a few hours off and get some rest, but she knew there just wasn't time. Doctor Vincent would need her help, and there were other patients to check up on as well.

"All right," she said, "let's go."

The instant the ward door shut behind them, the man's eyes flew open. He looked around the room as best he could without moving his head, just to be absolutely certain he and Etrec were alone.

With a slow, steady movement he raised himself to a sitting position and slid off the bed. He crossed to Etrec, who still slept, his face pale and smooth. As the man reached down and tenderly placed his hands on the young face he felt a great wave of sadness pass through him.

At the touch Etrec's eyes fluttered open, at first in fright and then with relief as he recognized the man. "Pasc!" he said happily. "Have they come back? Have they found a way?"

Pasc shook his head sadly. "We are among strangers. There is no way but our way."

The young boy's eyes widened in fear. "No, Pasc! No. Perhaps the strangers can help."

"There is no help for me. Soon there will be no help for you."

A thought crossed Etrec's mind, a dark memory of his fate, and he raised a hand questioningly to his forehead. Pasc gently pushed it away. "Not yet," he said.

Etrec felt a momentary relief. "Please don't let it come."

"I cannot stop it." He felt the glow as the flame emblem on his own forehead began to show itself.

"Yes, you can," insisted Etrec. "Kill me."

"No, I cannot."

"Why not? You killed Lok and Kerak."

A great inner agony passed over Pasc's features, and the symbol glowed even more brightly, a brilliant beacon of red heat. "I need you," he said despondently, "and the time is coming when you will have need of me." He turned away and eased himself back on his own bed. He carefully composed his emotions and could feel the scarlet sign fading away. He knew something would have to be done about that, very quickly. Then a roll of gauze bandage on the bedside table caught his eye.

When Helena heard that Commander Koenig would be radioing in to the Command Center in a few minutes, she rushed up to talk to him. Yasko and Tony were already trying to make contact when she arrived.

"Eagle One," said Yasko, "come in, Eagle One. Moon Base Alpha channel clear."

The big screen cleared, and slowly a picture of the pilot section of Eagle One came up on it. The reception seemed unusually bad, with the screen image constantly broken and sliced by lines of static. Several times it disappeared altogether.

"Eagle One to Moon Base Alpha. Are you receiving?" Koenig queried.

Yasko adjusted her controls to try to clear the video and audio receptions. "Not too well, Commander," she reported. "There's a lot of interference."

"I'm not surprised," he said. "We're being blitzed by a meteor storm. The survey team here have been hit bad. Lots of equipment damaged, and several men are trapped underground. We may lose contact with you, so let's wrap this up fast."

Tony cut in, looking worried. "I'll get another Eagle out to assist you if you want me to, Commander."

"Negative, Tony. Save the fuel. Maya and I can handle it all right. Now, is Helena there?"

Helena switched on her console so that Koenig could see her on the Eagle's receiver. "Here, John."

"Anything to add on our visitors yet?"

"They're still asleep. We're going to run a full med analysis. All tests up to now show them borderline human norm."

Koenig nodded. "Anything to add, Tony?"

"Planet unknown, Commander," he reported crisply. "No identification. Unable to interrogate yet. Until we can do that, they're an X factor."

With just the right note of warning, Koenig replied, "Until you do know, *treat* them as an X factor."

When the voice came, it startled them all, even Koenig, who heard it through the haze of radio disturbance. It was a voice with a peculiar carrying clarity, sonorous and strong as a tempered sword blade.

"And what would you like to know?" it asked.

All the personnel in the Command Center turned to face the man and the boy who had just come through the main doors. They were dressed in their plain, silver-colored, one-piece suits, and the older man had a turban-like swath of bandage around his head. Koenig could see them, too, once Yasko had the presence of mind to switch over to the wide-angle camera that took in the entire room.

As the two came down to stand beside Helena, Alan Carter got over his surprise and came running. "Hey, cobber!" he shouted and gently patted Etrec on the shoulder. He towered over the frail boy. "Glad to see you up and about."

Etrec was completely puzzled. "Cobber?" he asked.

Alan beamed at him. "It means you're a pal, a real close buddy." He winked. "Maybe you don't remember it but I'm the bloke that pulled you out from that blinkin' cave-in."

Etrec only began to vaguely understand what was being said to him, but felt a natural liking for the tall blond man anyway.

Pasc explained their recovery to Helena. "Our systems break down a sedative, as you put it, more quickly than yours."

"What about your head?" she questioned.

His face was blandly believable as he said, "Just a scratch. My equilibrium was not fully restored when I stood up. My head hit the wall."

Helena immediately reached up to lift the gauze and cast her professional eye on the wound. Pasc caught her hand gently, but firmly. "Please," he said, "I cannot allow you. A man's blood has a deep spiritual significance on Archanon."

Maya's voice came through the Center's speakers. "Archanon?" They looked up at the screen to see that she had joined Koenig in the view of the camera. "Archanon . . ." she said once again, thoughtfully, as if she were trying to remember.

Watching Maya, no one saw Pasc start with fear when he understood that someone had recognized the name of

his home planet. He quickly composed his face to hide h.
apprehension.

Maya suddenly recalled what she was searching for.
"It's the Planet of Peace," she announced.

Pasc felt a rush of relief. "Yes, we are Archanons, the
Peace-Bringers. I am Pasc and this is Etrec, my son."

"On Psychon," said Maya, "we picked up legends
from other space travellers . . . legends of the Peace-
Bringers . . . of the conquest of Evil by Good . . ."

Abruptly the picture on the big screen began to jump
and break up. A harsh rattle of sound replaced Maya's
voice and Yasko tried to reestablish contact on another
frequency.

"It's no use," said Tony, "we've lost them. Keep a
channel open. They'll get back to us when there's a break
in the storm."

Helena turned thoughtfully to Pasc. "The conquest
of Evil by Good?" she asked.

"Violence was outlawed on Archanon. We replaced
Evil with Good amongst our own people. Then we sent
emissaries throughout the universe so that others could
see that it could be done. I was the leader of such a
mission."

"From what we've learned of most of the races we
have come across so far," interjected Tony, "you didn't
have much success."

Pasc held up his hands in a gesture of concession. "It
takes time to reach all beings." His face became grimmer.
"It was not, however, until we reached your solar system
that we met with total failure. My mission ended on
your third planet . . . Earth. We had a base on the Moon
and observed. We saw such violence and hatred that
my wife, Lyra, begged me to leave Earth to its fate. I
overruled her. We descended. Like doctors entering a
plague area, we thought we were immune. We were not.
Only Etrec and I escaped contagion. When we returned
to our base on the Moon, the whole crew mutinied. We
were overpowered and placed in stasis, while the crew
took off to carry their madness . . ." he paused, "your
madness, to the farthest corners of the universe."

65

Silence reigned in the room after the grim tale had been recounted. Pasc's voice had made it all seem so immediate. Then Alan felt puzzled by something.

"Why the stasis chamber?" he asked. "Why didn't they kill you?"

Oddly Pasc smiled at the question, but it was a reaction of panic while he thought of a way to answer. "They could not," he said nervously.

"Do you mean Archanons cannot die?"

"The Archanons cannot kill . . . even in their sickness." As Pasc spoke Etrec moved closer to him, looking up with a haunted, uncertain expectation.

"But then, what is the sickness?" asked Helena.

Pasc cleared his throat and then looked away, as if he hadn't completely caught the question. "The taking of any kind of life," he said quickly, "is abhorrent, indeed impossible, for the race of Archanon."

"Your wife?" Helena tried to make the question sound gentle. "What happened to her?"

Pasc smiled wanly. "She led the mutineers. She put us in the chamber."

With a gasp Etrec suddenly collapsed, saved from crashing to the floor only by the quick reflexes of Tony. He held him under the arms and lowered him easily. Helena took the boy's arm and felt his pulse.

"Is he all right?" Alan asked anxiously.

Helena diagnosed, "Exhaustion, mostly. I'll have him taken to the sick bay."

"I'll take him," volunteered Alan, feeling a sharp twinge of concern for the youth. Having pulled him from underneath the cave-in had forged a strong bond of friendship, but also, Alan had always liked children. There weren't any on Moon Base, even though there were enough couples who were married or sufficiently in love to provide them. Koenig had ordered, and everyone had agreed, that childbirth should be avoided until the future of the Alphans was more secure.

In the Medical Section, Alan stayed close by while Helena ran another medical check. She turned to meet his inquisitive stare and shrugged.

"Nothing organically wrong," she said, "but there are still a few of the details of his physical structure that we don't understand yet."

"He doesn't look any different than any of us . . ."

"It's on the inside, Alan . . . the things we can't see with the naked eye. We'll take holograms, X-rays, a whole series of tests . . ."

Their attention was suddenly drawn to the bed where Etrec groaned and lifted his head off the pillow. His eyes were confused, bewildered.

"Hiyah, Cobber," said Alan, smiling, "how do you feel?"

Etrec gazed at him blankly for a moment, then returned a weak grin. "Hungry," he said.

Alan guffawed and turned to Helena. "You see, Doc, the only thing wrong with the kid is he hasn't had a square meal in a thousand years." He helped Etrec sit up and swing off the bed. "Now, listen . . . there's a little place just down the corridor. It's got hamburgers like you wouldn't believe."

"Hamburgers?"

"Well, so it's mixed with a little hydroponic soya . . . but it tastes like the real thing." Alan winked at Helena. "Okay with you, Doc?"

She nodded. "Just don't overdo it. Like you said, he hasn't eaten for a thousand years."

After Helena had left the room, Alan turned and watched Etrec take a few faltering steps away from the bed. He still seemed to be very shaky on his legs. Alan reached out an arm to him.

"Can you make it?" he said.

Neither of them noticed as Pasc slipped silently through the door into the room. In his hand he clutched a partially concealed surgical scalpel, and his eyes were fixed intently on Alan's back.

"I'll tell you what," Alan said to Etrec. "I'll carry you."

Etrec shook his head adamantly. "No. Please. I would rather walk."

As he looked up from the floor, Etrec saw past Alan where Pasc was stealthily approaching and could plainly read his intention in the expression on his face. He felt a terrible pull of loyalties, wondering how not to betray his father, but at the same time unable to stand by and watch his friend . . .

"Please," he said to Alan, reaching out.

Alan instantly bent down and gestured to his shoulders. "Just climb aboard the kangaroo and we'll get hopping."

As Etrec straddled him, Aaln stood up and turned. Pasc, thwarted by the intervention of his own son's body, had concealed the scalpel behind him and got his expression in control. Alan was startled to see him, but smiled amiably.

"We're just off for a bite to eat . . . want to join us?"

Pasc shook his head, not daring to try to speak. He could still feel a great knot of tension inside his chest . . . feel the hot pulse of the symbol concealed by the bandage. He watched Alan carry Etrec out of the room, his son glancing back for one tortured moment. Then he was alone, feeling only the cold deadliness of the scalpel up his sleeve.

CHAPTER SEVEN

The blood cell came into focus on the Medical Center's viewing screen, magnified thousands of times over. As the image cohered, Helena and Doctor Vincent could see every detail of the cell clearly. Helena could tell it wasn't a human blood cell by certain structural differences. Exactly how they would affect the organism that it came from, she didn't yet know. In any case, she was at the moment far more interested in a shape inside the cell's nucleus—it was like a star with tendrils trailing from each of its points.

"What do you think?" asked Doctor Vincent.

"No question about it. Even though it is Archanon blood, I feel certain that it's a virus. And look at the blurred effect at the tip of that tendril."

"Yes?"

"It means that the virus is still alive. Let's see Etrec's plate."

The picture on the screen changed and when focused was very similar to the first. This time the object with the nucleus was sphere-shaped with only the slightest points along its outside wall.

"It has every characteristic of the virus in the Pasc specimen, except it's not fully formed . . . and the tendrils are tiny."

"Could it be dead?" asked Doctor Vincent.

"Or dormant. We won't know until we isolate it and run some practical tests." She turned off the screen. "We'd better get them both in."

Andy Johnson walked purposefully down the corridor. Around the bend ahead of him he heard a strange and regular thumping sound, as if something soft and hollow was being punched hard. He was puzzled to see, as he stepped into the adjacent hallway, Etrec taking a short run. Abruptly he stopped and his foot drove into a round, brown object that Andy identified with surprise as a soccer ball.

Farther down the hallway, Alan Carter was crouching down. Just at the last second, as the ball was about to go past him on the left, he sprang sideways and gathered it in with one big hand. Dropping it to the floor he kicked it lightly and accurately back to Etrec.

"Remember . . . no hands!" Alan shouted. "Use your head or your feet!"

Etrec lunged and caught the ball with his forehead as it bounced and sent it back the way it had come.

"A good one!" Alan cheered.

This time Alan stopped the ball's roll with his toe and flipped it up so that he could bounce it again on his knee. As it hit the floor he chopped his instep into it vigorously so that it came down the hallway like a bullet. Andy ducked back around the intersection to keep from getting hit.

"Hey! That's a goal for me!" Alan shouted as Etrec failed to stop the shot. "Good try, though. A little more practice and we'll have you playing goalie for the Alpha Eagles."

As Etrec lined the ball up to kick it back, Andy stuck his head carefully around the corner again. "Excuse me, sir," he said to Alan.

"Hey, Bluey!" greeted Alan. "Just in time . . . you can be referee."

Andy walked across to Etrec and looked down at the battered sphere. Is that thing *real*?" he asked.

"*Real*!" Alan sounded outraged. "This is the ball that Wilkie used to score nine goals in Sydney Stadium in the Australian Cup Final in 1927!"

Johnson knew very little about soccer, and had in fact been more of a baseball player in his youth back on Earth. So he hadn't any idea how impressed he ought to be by Alan's boast. For politeness' sake, though, he looked awed. "You're kidding," he said.

Alan thrust the ball under his nose. "Look," he said, "there's Wilkie's signature, right there."

Etrec had obviously been treated to the full history of the ball as well, as he added brightly, "Alan's grandfather caught it in the stadium when he was about my size. It has been in his family ever since. And he would not let it out of his hands for a million . . . what was it you said, Alan?"

Alan touseled his hair. "For a million buckets of suds." He grinned at Andy. "You want to try and kick a few?"

Johnson suddenly remembered why he had been looking for Alan in the first place. "Oh, say . . . Tony wanted me to find you, to tell you we got the stuff out of the cavern."

"The stasis chamber and the power unit?"

"Yeah. The chamber is pretty well smashed to scrap, but the power unit is hardly touched. They've been taken to Tech Lab Three. Tony wanted you to come over there."

Alan dropped the ball and began to dribble it with his feet. "Let's go, then. Here ya go!" He passed the ball to Etrec, who ran to catch up with him.

The power unit had Tony and the technical team absolutely stumped. They had been going over it for hours, and it was still nothing more than a little black box with some dials and a few buttons on the front. The computer couldn't decode the few symbols that were inscribed on it, claiming insufficient information. They couldn't even fathom a way of getting it open so they could look at the inside.

When Alan and Etrec arrived, Tony shrugged and admitted failure. "Pasc is on his way down. We'll just have to wait."

"What about you, pal?" Alan asked Etrec. "You got the combination to the safe?"

Etrec caught the gist of the question and shook his head. "I hadn't got as far in my studies as the mechanics of energizers. I was still studying wave-particles analysis."

The technicians turned away to hid their smiles but felt impressed nonetheless. The door to the room hissed open just then, and Pasc came in wearing an expression of blank detachment.

"Father should know," volunteered Etrec helpfully.

Pasc lifted his eyebrows and shugged apologetically. "It's the same all over the universe . . . in the eyes of the son, the father is the infinite source of knowledge. And in this case, as in all others, their confidence is somewhat misplaced."

Etrec frowned. "But you knew all about . . ."

"As Commander of the expedition, I was merely co-ordinator. I had my specialists for this type of thing." Pasc started to turn away.

"How about opening it?" asked Tony quickly. "Surely you can at least show us how to work that."

71

There was an uncomfortable silence as Pasc hesitated. He seemed to be searching for something to say, but he couldn't quite think of it. He stepped across to the black box and placed his hands against two sides. As he pressed it carefully, the end of the box snapped open and gently eased down to reveal the interior.

Everyone gathered around for a closer look as Pasc reached inside. The small, complex nugget of crystals and wires he took out made him start so much he nearly dropped it.

"I know what that is!" Etrec said brightly. "It's a monitor transmitter."

Pasc cut him off. "Used in planetfall. To locate the unit and the team using it."

Tony peered at the small mechanism. "Yes. We have those . . . but they don't look anything like that." There was a note of suspicion in his voice. "Odd they left it in there unless they planned to come back sometime. What's its range?"

"I'm sure they weren't planning to come back," Pasc said brusquely, trying to deflect Tony's wariness. "It was just a standard component in the unit. The range, uh . . . well, it's whatever is required."

Pasc felt relieved when there was a bleep on Tony's comlock. He clicked on the miniature viewer and saw Helena. "Verdeschi," he acknowledged.

"Are Pasc and Etrec with you, Tony?" she asked.

"Yes."

"Please have them come over to Medical. Right away, please. It's important."

Tony felt reluctant to let them go. He had a deepening feeling that Pasc wasn't telling them all he knew and that a few careful questions might help him find out why. Besides, there were still some other components inside the box and at least Etrec could help name them, if nothing else.

Pasc suddenly seemed anxious to go, however, and pulled Etrec away by the shoulder. "If the good Doctor says it is important, we'd better go."

As soon as they were outside the lab and not in sight

of anyone, Pasc took a stronger grip on Etrec and pulled him quickly along beside him.

"Pasc!" Etrec protested. "It is not that way."

"We are not going to the Doctor. We have got to get away." He pulled him on even faster. "That monitor transmitter is set to the Archanon frequency. On Archanon they now know we are free."

"They will come for us?" Etrec asked in fright.

"But we will not be here!" Pasc answered fiercely. "We will take one of their Eagles and escape. Somewhere out there we will find a place and make it our own."

While they waited for the two Archanons to arrive at the Medical Center, Helena and Doctor Vincent ran through their brainwave pattern recordings again. Helena tapped her finger at certain points on the screen as the two patterns rolled past, side by side.

"There it is again!" she exclaimed. "You see how the pattern of Pasc's brain peaks unusually here, and here, but there's no corresponding movement in Etrec's."

"You think it could be connected with the virus?" asked Doctor Vincent. "Active in Pasc, dormant in the boy?"

"Their blood samples should help give us the answer." Helena reached over and pressed Tony's comlock code on the communication panel.

"Verdeschi," he said, coming into view on the screen.

"Tony, are Pasc and Etrec still with you?"

The surprise was plain on Tony's face. "No. They left for Medical when you asked them to. Aren't they there yet?"

"No."

"I'll get someone on it," Tony promised, and signed off.

There was barely time for Tony to get a message out to several security officers to start a search for the Archanons before he had a call from the Command Center. Yasko told him that Eagle One was trying to get a message through.

Up in the Command Center itself he came rushing in

73

just as Koenig's voice boomed out of the speakers, punctuated with harsh static. "Eagle One to Moon Base."

Yasko had the volume turned right up and was fighting hard to get a clearer frequency. Up on the big screen streaks of light flashed and scattered.

"Eagle One to Moon Base!" This time it was Maya's voice and Tony could just make out a hazy image of her on the screen.

"That's the best I can do," explained Yasko.

Tony leaned to the microphone. "Eagle One. Are you receiving?"

"Not very well, Tony."

"Do you want us to attempt to reach you?"

Koenig's voice came through. "No . . . storm is hitting peak. We can ride it out . . . too dangerous for another ship to try to get through. We're all right . . . we're . . ."

The communication was broken, and an overwhelming roar of static filled the room. Yasko sighed and switched off. Tony shrugged helplessly, but then an internal monitor bleeped for his attention.

"Yes, Alan?" he asked, as the Aussie's face clicked into view.

"I'm at Tech Lab Three with Johnson. We've had another go at this box and we think we've found some kind of recording device inside. If you're hooked into Eagle One we'd like to see if Maya can give us an opinion."

"We've lost contact. Will try to put you through if we regain."

Alan walked back to the table where the odd little box stood in a pool of directed light. Andy was moving around to look at it from the other side so that he wouldn't have to touch it. Since they had accidentally got the top panel to pop open, he didn't want to risk doing something that would make it close again.

The piece of the box that had opened was framing a matchbox-sized opaque oval and underneath it was a series of shiny metal rods slotted into vertical holes. Alan

74

reached down and carefully pulled one of them out for a closer look.

Andy scratched his head. "What makes you think it's some kind of recording device? It could be anything from an electronic pencil to a paperweight."

"It's just . . . well . . . that small panel there . . . it could be a screen. Kind of a hunch, I guess."

Johnson took the rod from Alan's hand and looked at it himself. At one end it was concave and at the other convex. Apart from that it had nothing particular about it at all. He tried to slip it back in the hole it had come from, but it didn't go all the way down.

Alan smirked and pulled it out again. "You just lack the right finesse, Bluey." He had noticed that all the other rods were showing the hollowed end up, and Andy had put that end down. He dropped it in the right way and pressed it securely down.

Suddenly the little screen glared with light and a miniature video picture of Pasc began to project. His recorded voice crackled through a concealed speaker.

"Four zero two, eight, two seven," Pasc's voice said mysteriously. "Entering small solar system in sector GL, three three, K. Third planet showing indications of primitive life forms."

"Hey!" exclaimed Andy. "You've done it, Alan! It's a data bank!"

They were distracted by footsteps approaching the lab door. Turning around they saw Carson, one of the security guards, smiling at them, with Pasc and Etrec following close behind.

"Is Mister Verdeschi still here?" Carson asked. "I located our friends. They got lost on the way over to Medical and I found them wandering around all the way over near the Eagle hangars . . ."

Carson's smiling explanation was cut off as Johnson came rushing across the room. "Mister Pasc!" he yelled. "I'm glad you're here. You've got to see this!"

"Doctor Russell wants them," protested Carson.

Alan motioned that it was all right. "We'll get them to Medical, Carson. You can push off."

75

Carson nodded. "Thanks, that's fine with me. I've been tailing around everywhere, and my feet are killing me." He gave a wave and walked off.

Very cautiously Pasc walked into the lab and toward the table with the box on it. "What have I got to see?" he asked Andy.

"This . . ." Andy moved to the box and reached down to press the rod again. "Let's have a replay."

The blow came as a complete surprise, crashing into the back of his head and slamming his face into the table. There was an explosion of lights and then a rushing wave of cold, cold blackness as he collapsed to the floor. He was certainly not conscious as his skull cracked sickeningly down.

Alan didn't know why Pasc had done it, but he reacted quickly, moving to restrain him. Pasc was ready, though, and grabbed him by the throat in a powerful double-handed clutch. They wrestled backward, kicking over a chair and thudding painfully against the wall.

Alan felt his awareness going, his eyes bulging in their sockets, and a roaring in his ears. Somewhere Etrec's voice yelled sharply, telling Pasc to stop. He reached desperately for Pasc's head and his anxious fingers caught in the bandage and ripped it away. Revealed beneath was the bright and horrific red symbol of the flame on Pasc's forehead.

With strength made great by fright, Alan broke the Archanon's grip and stumbled to the communication panel. He punched down the emergency button, but as he turned again, Pasc moved in and punched heavily into his chest. With the breath knocked out of him and his brain still in an orange fog from his near strangulation, Alan could hardly raise his arms to protect himself.

Etrec clung desperately to his father, trying to stop him from swinging again, but he wasn't strong enough. Pasc raised one arm high up and brought it sharply down so that his fist crashed right on top of Alan's head. The Australian's body dropped as though pole-axed.

"You've killed him!" screamed Etrec.

The alarm siren began to wail, activated by the Command Center in response to the emergency signal from the lab. Pasc looked around in panic, feeling the very walls pulse with danger to him. On his forehead the terrible emblem was as bright as fire.

CHAPTER EIGHT

By the time Tony and several security guards got to the Technical Laboratory Number Three, there was no one there to greet them except the prone forms of Alan and Andy. The alert siren was screeching away relentlessly throughout the base, and it was this as much as anything that was bringing Alan back to consciousness.

"What's happened?" Tony asked, shaking him into alertness.

Alan tried to clear his throat to speak, but for some reason it was very painful; even his breath hurt going down. There was also a ridge of agony across the top of his head ... then he remembered. Looking around quickly, he saw that the Archanons had gone, but that Andy was still sprawled next to the table. A security man had just stood up from his side, his hand red from the pool of blood that was spreading on the floor.

"Andy ...?" Alan forced the question out.

The security man shook his head. "He's dead, Mister Carter."

"It was Pasc," Alan told Tony, sorrow adding to the difficulty of speech. "He attacked us both."

Tony clicked on his comlock. "Verdeschi to Medical Center!"

Helena received the message and acknowledged it.

"Casualty at Tech Lab Three. Get over here fast, Doctor." Then as soon as Helena said she was on her way, Tony called back to the Security Section Office. "Verdeschi to Security. Full Alert. Locate the alien man Pasc. He is to be considered extremely dangerous. Use extreme caution . . . but get him!"

Tony sent the security men in the lab out to help with the search and then assisted Alan to get to his feet. As soon as his head stopped spinning, he showed Tony what he and Andy had discovered about the black box and described how Pasc had attacked them. Then, grimly, he described the symbol on Pasc's forehead that had been hidden underneath the bandage.

Tony couldn't offer any suggestions about the symbol's significance but felt an instinctive dread concerning it. He was anxious to go off and join the search and suggested Alan wait in the lab until Helena arrived and could check him over.

"Not bleeding likely," he said. "He's got the lad with him. I'm coming with *you*."

They started along the corridor that led toward the travel tube that Helena would have used to get over from the medical area. If she had come right away, she really should have arrived by then. Why she hadn't was puzzling until they stepped around a corner and were stunned by a scene that seemed to answer most of the immediate mysteries.

Helena, eyes wide with fright, was being held forcibly from behind by Pasc, who had a handgun aimed at her head. One security guard was standing helplessly by and another, evidently the man whom Pasc had taken the weapon from, was collapsed on the floor. Etrec stood just behind him, his face creased by distress.

"Pasc!" Tony shouted in alarm.

Etrec looked across and saw that Alan had arrived with Tony. His face brightened, and he ran over before Pasc could stop him.

"Cobber!" the boy called out. "I thought he had killed you."

78

Pasc shouted angrily. "Etrec! Come back! Come here by me!"

Etrec looked back and once again was filled by the pull of divided loyalties. He took a faltering step toward his father.

Suddenly Tony reached out and grabbed the boy's shoulder in a firm clasp. At the same time he drew his gun and raised it to Etrec's head. "Let the woman go," he said to Pasc, "or I will kill the boy."

There was an electric silence in the room. Alan was appalled by Tony's words and silently reached over to touch Etrec's arm. Pasc saw the gesture and laughed . . . a harsh and cruel sound.

"You cannot do it," he mocked. "The killing is not in you. But I can . . . and I *will*, unless you let him go."

Tony tried to stare him down, but the glare of madness in Pasc's eyes was too strong. He could see the Archanon's fingers straining on the grip of the gun and could also clearly see that it was set on the killing laser beam, not the stun ray. He gave up and let Etrec go.

Pasc laughed viciously again. "Now listen. We are taking one of the Eagles. Get your men away from the flight area and have an Eagle standing by for us."

Tony reluctantly issued the order through his comlock. When it was acknowledged, he nodded to Pasc.

"Etrec," instructed Pasc, keeping his firm hold on Helena, "you lead the way."

Etrec started to walk, head hanging low. Then he stopped and looked back at Alan Carter. "No, Pasc," he said quietly, still looking at Alan, "I am not going."

"You cannot stay here," Pasc snapped. "They are your friends now, but soon they will have to kill you . . . for their own safety."

"Then it will have to be. I am staying."

"Then I will kill you myself!" Pasc roared, and aimed the gun at the boy. The symbol on his head began to throb with scarlet, and his mouth twisted into a grimace of hatred.

Etrec waited calmly for the shot, but Pasc's arm faltered and fell. Very cautiously Tony began to raise

79

his own weapon, hoping for a chance to stun the Archanon, but froze as the man put the gun back to Helena's head. He began to move backwards down the corridor, pulling Helena with him. The travel tube, doors open, waited, dumbly obedient and ready to speed them away.

Inside the Eagle, Pasc made Helena take the co-pilot's seat. Some of the mechanisms for operating the craft were primitively obvious to him . . . but others he would have to make her explain. If she couldn't, they would take a little longer to understand, but he would manage in the end. As long as he kept her hostage, then time was on his side.

Turning to Helena he caught her looking at him warily, but also with a hint of knowing something about him that he didn't suspect. He didn't like the feeling.

"I should have killed him," he said.

Helena asked, "Why didn't you?"

"He chose to stay. I chose survival." Pasc looked back at the controls . . . the great puzzle board of dials, buttons, switches, and screens.

"There may not be survival for either of you, Pasc," Helena said evenly, significantly.

Pasc understood that she was hinting at what she thought she knew about him. "What makes you speak thus," he asked.

"I saw into your brain, Pasc. We took pictures when you were under sedation . . . your brain and Etrec's brain . . . There is a strange virus in your systems. In Etrec it seems to be dormant—for the moment." She paused and took a deep breath. "Not with you, Pasc. Yours is alive. It may be deadly. It's why I wanted samples of blood from both of you . . . to try to know what it is."

A faint glow began to emanate from Pasc's forehead, and his eyes burned with murder. He felt himself outraged by her presumption . . . her feeble attempt to help those who were beyond redemption. His hand tightened on the gun, but he also knew that he still had use for her as a hostage.

"Enough talking!" he said. "Show me how to work the communication device."

Inside the Command Center a state of severe emergency was in effect. Tony had gathered the Security Section's officers and was briefing them on tactics.

"I want all men in protective suits. There'll be a team of sharpshooters with stunners and anesthetic gas guns—" Tony broke off as he saw Alan come striding through the door from the corridor. Alan had just taken Etrec down to the recreation room to keep him out of the way of danger . . . and to avoid distressing him with whatever they might have to do to rescue Helena.

"Alan," Tony called over to him, "we've got to get aboard that ship without alerting Pasc." Reaching down to the master control panel he summoned from the computer a diagram of an Eagle's layout. He pointed to a section of the illustration. "Through the cargo hatch?" he asked.

"No," advised Alan. "It's too noisy. He'd be warned before we could get in and have the advantage."

"Hmmm . . . for the same reason drilling through the hatch or the hull is out. What about acid?"

"The most powerful acid we have would take nearly three hours to eat through an Eagle hull."

Despondently they continued to study the Eagle design, feeling only too certain that it was in vain. Alan knew the inside and outside of the craft as well as he knew the palm of his hand. There just wasn't any way to get at Pasc unless they could bluff him into letting them come on board or get him to come out. And how much time they had to do either of those depended on how long it was before he took off.

The big screen suddenly flickered to life, showing all of the Eagle's pilot section interior. Pasc glared just as fiercely as before, but there was some relief for them in seeing that Helena was still unharmed.

"This is Pasc speaking," the Archanon announced coldly. "I want Etrec in exchange for your Doctor."

81

Alan spoke brusquely back to him. "Etrec made his choice. He didn't want to go with you."

Pasc scowled and raised a menacing fist. "I have neither patience nor time! Bring the boy to me, or I will kill the woman! It will not take me many minutes to master the controls of this vessel. I will give you only until I do . . . then she dies!"

Before Pasc could break off the communication, Helena leaned forward and began urgently to speak. "Tony, get Ben Vincent! Tell him to—" The screen went dead.

Neither Tony nor Alan could guess what it was that Helena wanted them to ask Doctor Vincent. But the brief communication had done one thing: made them more certain than ever that Helena was in mortal peril. Tony clicked a channel through to the Medical Center.

"We just had a call from Pasc in the Eagle, Ben. He wants to make a deal . . . swap Helena for the boy."

Doctor Vincent looked doubtful, his distrust of the offer very obvious.

"Helena tried to say something," Alan added. "She wanted us to ask you to do something, but Pasc cut her off. What do you think she wanted?"

Pondering the possibilities, Doctor Vincent sucked at his lower lip. "I'm not sure. Could've been something to do with the virus we think we found that Pasc and the lad are apparently carrying. We've been hoping to get blood samples from them to test. Maybe Helena caught onto something from Pasc."

Tony turned to Alan. "Right," he said slowly and gravely, "it's up to you. Etrec trusts you. You've got to get a blood sample from him and then get him to co-operate in an exchange . . . *and* you've got to do it fast."

It was very clear that Alan wasn't feeling happy about any of it, but he also understood that the first priority was to save Helena's life. He could recall some times when his own life had depended on her help. Indicating he would try his best, he turned glumly away.

Etrec was alone in the recreation center and gradually he had been drawn to the end of the room where a small aviary held a pair of plump, white doves. They had cooed to him softly as he watched them through the bars of the cage. All the time he stood there he had felt an oddly growing feeling ... like icy cold fingers reaching up over the back of his brain.

When Alan came into the room, he shouted to Etrec's back, "Hey, mate. How're you doing?"

Taken by surprise, Etrec was suddenly jolted out of a kind of thoughtless daydream. He was confused to see that he had taken one of the doves from the cage and was tightly squeezing it in his hands. Appalled, he let go, and the frightened bird shot up and flew in swift circles around the large room. It finally came to roost on the rail above the cinema screen.

"They're not usually let out," Alan said easily, "but never mind. It'll fly back home when it's time to eat."

Etrec hardly heard the words, so intensely aware was he of a deep, pulsing heat just above his eyes. He kept facing away from Alan, horror-struck with the realization of just what was happening to him.

"Look, cobber," Alan said gently. "We've got big problems and big decisions. Pasc has told us that he still wants you to go with him, and unless—"

"I don't want Pasc!" Etrec cut in sharply. "He's my father ... but I don't want him the way he is." He moved farther away from Alan to keep his face concealed.

"Pasc told us he will kill the Doctor unless he gets you back ..."

The voice of Etrec became even harsher and trembled with uncommon emotions. "He will kill her anyway! He can't help it. Neither of us can! We have the Archanon killing sickness!"

Very quickly things began to fall into place for Alan. He felt that another few clues might unlock the entire horrible mystery. "Etrec," he urged, "Helena wanted to tell us something. Pasc wouldn't let her. Doctor Vincent thinks she wanted him to get a sample of your blood ... that it has something to do with your sickness."

Next to Etrec was a rack which held various trays of cutlery for personnel to use when they came into the recreation room to eat. In the tray on the end he could see light gleaming off the sharp points and serrated edges of some knives. The deadly efficiency of the steel's shape and texture tantalized his eye.

"An Archanon cannot give his blood." Etrec's voice was distant ... distracted.

Alan moved closer to him, pleading. "Look, I'm no doctor. I don't even know what they're talking about ... but this could be a good thing. It might save your life ... Pasc's ..."

This time Etrec was more adamant. "An Archanon cannot give his blood! It is impossible!"

Not understanding what Etrec meant ... thinking perhaps there was some religious or racial custom involved, Alan still tried to persuade him. He was stunned when the youth spun around to face him, growling like an animal. In his hand he clutched a knife, and on his forehead the flame symbol was growing brighter and brighter.

Alan held his ground and spoke with deliberate quietness. "Do you think you can kill *me*, cobber?"

Etrec jerked the knife up and held it overhead, the blade trembling with the anticipation of plunging into flesh. In Alan's calm and steady eyes, Etrec could see a reflection of the light striking off the sharp steel. His arm ached to move ... to strike out and spend its energy in swift violence.

The agony of the moment seemed as though it would never end, but at last, Etrec could stand the competing pressures of emotion no longer. The deep bond of friendship ... the newly bloomed compulsion to inflict death ... he screamed and brought the knife savagely down.

Alan was more appalled at what Etrec did than if the lad had actually stabbed *him* with the knife. Instead the blade flashed straight against the dreaded emblem that burned under Etrec's skin, ripping into the flesh and bouncing off the bone below it. The startling pain made Etrec drop the knife to the floor but also seemed to clear his thoughts. The psychotic possession fled from his mind in the face of the damage he had just inflicted on himself.

"You asked for Archanon blood," he said softly. "It

is yours." His eyes rolled upward and he fell limply.

Alan managed to catch him before he hit the floor and supported him against one knee as he whipped out his comlock. He wanted to let Ben know he was bringing Etrec over and that he had plenty of blood to take a sample from. It streamed brightly from the dreadful wound.

In the Command Center Tony paced nervously. Apart from stationing security men near the Eagle's airlocks, there was nothing else he could do. Yasko was working desperately, on his instructions, to try to contact Koenig in Eagle One. He had almost told her to stop trying; the storm was obviously still raging.

"Sir," Yasko said curiously, "I'm getting a signal . . . but . . ."

"The Commander?" Tony blurted, hurrying over.

"No." Her eyes widened in surprise. "I think it's alien!"

All eyes looked up to the big screen as the radio signal directed telescopic cameras to search the sector of space where the signal had originated. Tony switched on a channel for audio response to the frequency on which the signal came, but before he could speak, a strange voice hummed over the receiver.

"Moon Base Alpha. Moon Base Alpha. Can you hear me?" The voice was feminine, and compellingly gentle.

"This is Moon Base Alpha. Who are you?"

Into view on the screen a strange spacecraft approached. It was streamlined and long with silvery green lights rippling along its curved sides. The image lasted only a moment and was replaced by video transmission of the possessor of the soothing voice. Tony recognized her at once as being an Archanon, but with an expression of friendliness and gentleness that was deeply sincere.

"Permission to land, Alpha?" the lady requested.

"Identify yourself, please," Tony insisted.

"I am Maurna," the lady said softly. "I am from Archanon. We have been receiving monitor transmissions that have informed us that two Archanons have been freed from restraint. We are concerned for your safety."

Tony nodded. There was something so gentle in the

voice but compellingly convincing. "Right now, one of them is holding one of our people hostage."

"And the other?"

"He is with us and seems to be all right, so far. But we must persuade him to join the other—Pasc, aboard one of our space craft, or else the hostage will be killed."

The look of dismay on the Archanon lady's face was heart-rending to see. It was obvious that the sense of revulsion at even the mention of violence ran very deeply. "You must let us deal with Pasc," she said emphatically.

Tony knew he had nothing to lose. Alan hadn't contacted him yet, so it was likely the boy couldn't be persuaded to go with his father . . . and time was running out. "Permission to land," he acknowledged.

Seconds after he broke contact with the Archanon ship, Tony's internal communications signal beeped for his attention. Alan's face was deeply etched with worry as he appeared on the screen and explained what had happened in the recreation room. Tony told him he would come over to the medical center right away.

"One other thing, Tony," Alan added before he could sign off. "I've got that Archanon black box over here with me. I've been trying some of the other memory rods. One of them seems to have all the answers."

"I'll be right there." Tony switched off and started toward the door. "When the Archanons arrive," he said to Yasko, "have them brought down to the Medical Center."

Alan had the little box with its screen all set up when Tony arrived. Tony watched and listened as Alan activated the memory rod with growing astonishment. Then he surprised Alan by telling him that a delegation of Archanons would be there momentarily.

"We've got to let Pasc know . . . that *we* know," Alan urged.

Tony agreed. "But don't say anything about the Archanon ship yet."

Alan moved the black box over the medical section's

communications panel and signalled the Eagle that he wanted to speak.

Pasc appeared immediately. "So you have come to your senses," he said. "You have Etrec? Bring him to me and you can have your Doctor back."

"One moment, Pasc," said Alan. "I want you to see something first."

Alan relayed the black box's memory recording so that it went through to the Eagle at the same time as they watched and listened to it again. A sad-faced Archanon woman of about Pasc's age appeared and began to speak.

"RO two—one one—one. It has happened again . . . that which we of Archanon dread above all." As much as she was trying to make the report clinically official, the emotion was strong in her voice. "The terrible scourge we thought we had eradicated from our genes has returned. Pasc has the killing sickness. Lok and Kerak are dead, wantonly destroyed by Pasc in the meaningless violence that this disease engenders in its victims. I, Lyra, have taken command. Pasc has been overpowered. I have ordered the preparation of a stasis chamber. We who remain cannot take life, not even in circumstances such as these. Pasc, therefore, will be placed in stasis, where he will remain until a cure for the killing sickness can be found." The voice of Lyra shook with tragedy as she continued, tears welling up in her eyes and trickling unheeded down her cheeks. "Since it is known that the killing sickness is passed on in the genes of the male line, I have . . . I have no alternative but . . . but to place in stasis, with Pasc, my . . . my son, Etrec. I . . . I pray that one day, he will be able to give me his forgiveness and understanding."

As the image faded, Pasc came back on the screen, his face a mask of grief and sorrow. "So now you know . . ." he said. "Where is Etrec? Let me see him."

Alan switched on a video camera so that Pasc could see Etrec lying unconscious on a hospital couch . . . his face pale and his breath faltering.

"What have you done to him?" Pasc shouted.

"Nothing," explained Alan. "He gave us his blood."

"You took Etrec's blood?" Pasc was horrified.

"He gave it himself, Pasc. He gave it freely. We have tested a specimen and we've confirmed that the virus can be cured. We can develop a serum, if—"

Helena abruptly interrupted. "What is the matter with Etrec?"

"Doctor Vincent says it's very unusual . . . it seems that he is incapable of replacing the blood he has lost."

"It is over," Pasc said slowly. "He is dying. There is nothing left now . . . nothing left."

The communication went dead.

Helena nervously watched Pasc as he slumped despondently in the pilot's seat. The news that Etrec had given his blood seemed to have broken him. She waited to see what he would do next, but he acted as though he had forgotten she was there.

Abruptly, without looking at her, he said softly, "I have lost Etrec. You may go."

"Pasc, listen . . ." she reached over and touched his arm. "Etrec doesn't have to die. You can give him a blood transfusion."

"My blood? With the active virus?"

"Yes! And that's exactly why. We'll prepare a serum from your blood that will cure him at the same time you replace what he has lost. You can save him if you want to!"

Pasc stiffened his arm under Helena's hand. "I do not save life. I take it!"

"No, Pasc. Not your own son's. You could not do it before. You cannot do it now."

Pasc shook his head adamantly. "No . . . I must take life! I must!"

Very much aware that time was crucial to Etrec's life, Helena argued even more forcibly, trying to ignore the fact that if she pushed Pasc into a fit of violence there was no longer any reason for him not to kill her. "You *can* have control. If you say you can't, it's only because you're afraid. Because you and your people have accepted it all these generations ... and whenever one just accepts, Pasc, no matter how advanced a race of people thinks it is, there can be no control. But fight it ... you can cure it. Give your blood for the serum and prove you don't accept the sickness."

Pasc buried his face in his hands with an agonized cry. "It is too late, I tell you. He cannot be saved!"

"Coward!" yelled Helena.

Pasc knocked her hand away viciously and looked at her with rage in his eyes. Helena held his stare, her own eyes challenging. "All right," he said stonily. "All right. Let's go, then."

When the message came through from Yasko that the Archanon ship had landed, Tony was pacing nervously in the hospital's emergency ward. Etrec and Pasc both lay nearby on treatment couches, and Doctor Vincent had injected the boy with the last of the serum that he had hastily prepared.

Helena hurried to the boy's side and took a sample blood smear on a micro-plate. They all gathered around the viewing screen as she put the sample under the microscope for computer-amplified magnification. It was clearly evident that the shape of the virus in the cell nucleus had shrivelled even further and would soon disappear altogether. Doctor Vincent nodded his satisfaction.

"It's working," he confirmed. "The virus is being destroyed." He looked across at the monitors for Etrec's other life functions. "The boy is picking up. Heart and blood pressure constantly improving."

Helena checked the readings herself and then walked over and switched off the transfusion pump. Etrec was doing well, but she was worried about the severity of the effect on Pasc. The reading on his body system was declining unexpectedly.

"Pasc is getting worse," she said to Doctor Vincent. "Stimulators."

With a weak smile, Pasc opened his eyes. "A waste of time," he said quietly. "The heart will not pump what is not there." His eyes flicked questioningly side-ways. "How is my son?"

"The virus is destroyed. He is a true Archanon again ... a Peace-Bringer."

Pasc smiled for real ... the first genuine smile Helena could remember him giving. "Good. Good. Lyra will be happy."

"Save your strength now," Helena told him. "In a few days we can increase the potency of the serum and start treating you."

Pasc closed his eyes again, saying, "No, that will not be necessary."

Etrec was beginning to breathe deeply, still asleep but strengthening all the time. The door slid open and Maurna came in, followed by two Archanon men. She looked at the scene in bewilderment.

Sensing something different in the room, Pasc opened his eyes again. Through a haze he saw Maurna standing over him. "Lyra?" he asked hopefully.

"No, Pasc," she said gently. "Lyra is gone these thousand years. I am Maurna ... but of Lyra's line."

"Peace to you, Maurna. I give into your care your kinsman, Etrec. Take him with you back to Archanon."

"You know I cannot, Pasc. There is still no place on Archanon for the sickness."

Helena stepped closer and spoke so that Pasc was sure to hear her. "Etrec no longer has the sickness. We prepared a serum from the blood of Pasc."

Maurna looked staggered. "Given freely?" The two Archanon men standing behind her whispered anxiously to each other.

Pasc said firmly, "Yes. Given freely."

"I can assure you," Helena intervened, "the cure is complete."

Maurna acknowledged that she believed her. "We know of the process on Archanon."

"You mean you could have cured Pasc ... and you didn't?"

Maurna realized that the Doctor didn't fully under-stand the significance of what had happened. "We knew of the cure," she explained, "but we could not use it. The Archanons do not have the necessary enzymes in their blood to replace what is lost. None of us could give the amount necessary for a transfusion and live ourselves."

Grim realization washed over Helena's face. She knew then that Pasc was dying and could not be saved. The pulse rate began to fade even as she looked down at him.

"It is the last privilege of the killing sickness . . ." he said feebly, "to kill oneself." His head rolled to one side in the direction where Etrec was resting peacefully on the other couch. But his eyes could not longer see . . . and death took him.

Maurna motioned to the other Archanons to come forward. "We will take Etrec home now," she said, "and Pasc, too. We thank you for what you have done."

Helena nodded and turned away to hide her own sadness. Maurna watched as Pasc's body was wrapped to be taken away. She was glad Etrec had not had to see his passing.

"Uhmmm." Alan stepped beside Maurna and held out his football to her. Her eyebrows raised in surprise at the scuffed, brown sphere. "This is for Etrec," Alan said. "He'll understand. Tell him his cobber said goodbye."

Carefully Maurna took the object, holding it with the sort of reverence that she suspected it must deserve. "I will tell him," she said.

CHAPTER NINE

Patrick Osgood stood in the center of the tunnel and in his white coverall suit looked more like a larger-than-life statue of a man than a real one. Everything about him had a stone-like hardness; there was a monolithic rigidity in his nature that made him both respected and feared among the men who worked with him.

A team of these stood nearby, about ten yards back in the tunnel from Osgood. There was only emergency lighting at this level ... the lowest of all the man-made tunnel systems beneath Alpha Moon Base. With the assistance of small lamps on their helmets, the team was checking their position on a map.

Some of the geological surveys had led mining teams farther afield to explore the Moon's own natural caverns in the search for tiranium. Osgood had elected to lead his team straight down ... knowing that the closer to the Moon's core they could get, the greater was the likelihood of locating the precious element.

Most of the tunnels through which they had explored had been planned to eventually house a greatly expanded Alpha Moon Base, back in the times before the fateful day that Luna broke away from Earth orbit. Now only the topmost levels were in use. On Koenig's orders most of the Moon Base sections had been transferred just below the surface for added protection from the dangers of deep space.

Osgood turned and walked back to his crew, his own doubts about the next step in the search resolved. His face was dark, with heavy brows and a thickly woven beard. Intense, ebony eyes burned out from each side of a nobly shaped, though broken, nose.

"I want some more charges ..." His deep voice reverberated in the tunnel as he reached out a big hand and stabbed locations on the map, "Placed here, here, here, and here."

Several of the men shook their heads doubtfully, frowning with concern. Osgood looked resolutely at each of them, seeking their confidence with only the firmness of his expression.

"I know we'll find it this time," he said. "I have faith!"

Osgood's first assistant felt very reluctant to question the plan, understanding how much finding tiranium meant to the big man personally...but he couldn't ignore his professional responsibility.

"Isn't it a bit risky, Chief? You put that many charges along that line there and..."

"Our job is to find tiranium in these catacombs," Osgood interrupted.

"We've already weakened the roof," the man persisted. "It's a pretty treacherous rock formation just there."

Osgood laid a fatherly hand on the assistant's shoulder, giving a reassuring squeeze. "Every rock formation we've come across in the Moon has been tricky. We must take risks in order to succeed...and this time we will. We *must!*"

They all knew there was no arguing with him and turned away to prepare the charges. Osgood took a deep breath and put away the map. If this attempt didn't bear fruit, they would have to give up the search. They didn't have the right kind of equipment to go any deeper.

When the satchels with their radio-activated blasting caps were ready, Osgood reached out and silently took them all...holding the weight easily over one arm. He turned and started off down the tunnel.

"Hey, Chief," one of the crew called after him. "You're not taking those down by yourself?"

"Yes!" Osgood's voice thundered. "All of you move farther back!"

"But, Chief..." the first assistant protested, "that hypernitro is touchy as anything. You shouldn't handle it by yourself. Just the slightest bump and..."

"Move back!"

The way Osgood stalked away made the satchels on his arm swing to and fro and bump together. Just watching it made most of the crew break out in a cold sweat. Quickly they gathered up their equipment and headed back to the lift shaft that connected with the next higher level.

"The Chief sure don't act like himself no more," one of the men said as they moved through the roughly hewn tunnel.

"If your wife was dying," the first assistant snapped edgily, "you wouldn't be yourself, either!"

Osgood felt confident that he was doing the right thing. They had been too cautious so far, and the standard strength of charges already in place along the tunnel wall would have given them yet another disappointment. With the addition of the explosives he was carrying they could be sure of a breakthrough.

So caught up in his burning rhapsody of faith was he, Osgood didn't realize he had reached the tunnel end until he nearly walked into it. The beam of his headlamp seemed to be fighting a losing battle against the overwhelming darkness. He could just make out the scars in the rock of earlier, unsuccessful explosions.

More attentively, he began to backtrack, sitting the new charges at midpoints between those already in place. He anticipated the blast would collapse the wall of the tunnel nearly twenty yards in a northerly direction, right into the strata that seismographic readings told them was the most likely arrangement for tiranium deposits.

As he placed the explosives his sense of urgency began to build up again. He thought desperately of his wife, feeling the full weight of the knowledge that her survival depended on him. He had to succeed . . . he *had* to!

He had nearly reached his starting point, with only one satchel left. Much less burdened, he was hurrying as much as he could, his massive shoulders stooped and just brushing the tunnel roof. Even if he had been fully concentrating on what he was doing, it was unlikely the brightness of his headlamp would have allowed him to see the rock in his path in time.

He felt it start to roll under his boot and knew that his forward speed was too great to keep from falling. The last bag of delicate hypernitro was still cradled in his arms and if he landed on it, the force was bound to set it off. He didn't have to think about it . . . he *knew*. With great strength, he twisted in mid-sprawl. The satchel was safely cradled against his chest as he landed heavily on his back, feeling the agony of large stone fragments digging into him.

Lying there, looking up at the pool of light that his headlamp threw on the roof, he cursed his own carelessness. The pains in his back began to subside, and his heartbeat slowed from its racing. Suddenly, he realized with a start, there was a whirring noise coming from right underneath him. At first he was mystified, but then he remembered that he had gone off from his team in such a hurry that he was still carrying the remote control detonation transmitter with him. It was in his back pocket, and when he fell he had set it off.

It was as if his intestines were suddenly filled with ice, reacting to the gruesome fear that the bag he hugged so close to his chest was about to erupt and scatter him into a million moist pieces. Fortunately, Osgood was a courageous man. That didn't mean that he didn't feel fear as much as the next man, but he didn't let that feeling stop him from doing something about it.

The distant thump of a concussion and the tense vibration through the ground confirmed the thought that had already raced through his mind. The blasts were set in series, from the deepest to the one closest to the mining crew. The one he held would be last to blow ... but the difference was only seconds. The blasts were coming steadily closer, like a giant running.

Osgood slid the satchel off and scrambled up, feeling stones shaking loose and pelting him as the floor danced crazily below. He ran, head down and arms pumping, making his legs drive with all their might. The roar of the blasts was growing to a horrific volume. He roared back at it, running, running with all his strength. Finally the tunnel filled with light, in its brilliance *became* light, and he was picked up and hurled through the air. He flew ... sailed like a bird down the illuminated column into beautiful silence.

The circle of light ahead of him blurred and began to change its character ... becoming firstly a milky disc. Features began to emerge as areas darkened and shadows tightened into sharp definition. Osgood floated closer ... coming down ... down. He was descending gently toward the face of the Moon. The unmistakable Mares and craters spread out underneath him in a silvery glow.

His feet touched the surface without a trace of a jolt, just slipping easily into the lunar sand. In front of him, about a hundred yards away, he could see a large, antique brass bed. There was a person lying on the floral print sheets that covered it, and even at that distance he knew it was his wife . . . Michelle.

Osgood began to walk forward . . . anxiously happy to be by his wife's side. He had taken only four strides when the sky above gasped. He looked up and saw a gigantic web of flames . . . like a great bramble bush on fire . . . falling toward the Moon.

He started running, shouting his wife's name as his feet fought for purchase in the loose sand. Early fragments of the fire were already landing, hissing like vipers as they dropped to the ground. To one side he could see some outbuildings of the Moon Base and as a very large knot of fire hit them they exploded into an inferno.

He looked back ahead of him to see that the bed was now encircled with bright fire. In its center, Michelle still lay quietly, her eyes closed.

"Michelle!" he yelled.

This time she heard him and sat up. Her long shiny hair fell loosely around her shoulders and her wide, doe-like eyes looked anxiously for him.

"Patrick? Oh, Patrick, is it you?" she cried.

"Yes, Michelle! Rise up and come to me. I can save us!"

Michelle struggled, but fell helplessly back to the bed . . . little fingers of fire climbing up the sheets and beginning to reach for the frilly edges of her white nightgown. "I haven't enough faith!" she cried in despair.

"I have enough for us both!" Osgood shouted, then plunged into the howling flames.

The crew's number one was the first to reach Osgood after they had dug through the rock fall. It was amazingly lucky, the way the long splinter of rock had fallen diagonally across his body, and had deflected all the other rubble.

Quarrying in the disused levels of the Moon Base for the rare and much-needed element Tiranium is not without its dangers for this unfortunate miner—especially when Osgood, the chief miner, appears to have flipped his lid.

(opposite, top) While the battle takes place to save the miner from his dangerous delusions, Helena pleads with Koenig to release a vital portion of Tiranium needed for a heart transplant operation on Osgood's pretty wife.

(opposite, bottom) Beautiful Michelle Osgood, dying from a fatal heart condition—and the subject of her husband's visions which drive him to abstraction.

(above) On the bed of flames, the beautiful Michelle dies a thousand times in Patrick Osgood's tortured imagination—not only symbolic of her imminent death, but of the approaching fire storm that will consume the Moon Base.

(above) Even in the depths of unchartered space, millions of light years away from Earth, it is still possible to encounter a friendly fellow human— only the human, Captain Michael, has been murdered by Brian, his computer. And Brian has a plan for Koenig and Helena, too.

(opposite, top) Brian the Brain—with a few more nasty tricks up his console.

(opposite, bottom) Koenig and Helena receive an unpleasant surprise when they are subjected to this bizarre test of love by the crafty Brian.

(opposite, top) After the subterranean chamber of the Archanons has been discovered, an accident triggers off a cave-in.

(opposite, bottom) After more mining for Tiranium, the tomb-like chamber of the afflicted Archanons is discovered—buried deep in the bowels of the Moon.

(above) Cursed by the dreaded Mark of Archanon, Pasc, freshly out of his tomb, tries to satiate his lust for slaughter—starting with Alan Carter.

(top) Alpha is threatened by a strange storm of fire from space...or is it the delusions of a mad man?

With no uncertain intention, the human-looking automation from the planet Vega forces his attentions on Helena, in the hope of provoking the jealous Commander Koenig to violence—and so enable itself to be programmed in the strictly unlovely art of killing.

He rolled Osgood over and found that he was still breathing. There was considerable bruising on his face and a trickle of blood from the side of his mouth. Another man handed over the first aid kit, but abruptly Osgood's eyes flew open.

"Hold still," the first assistant ordered, thinking of the textbook routine to check for broken bones, internal damage, shock.

Osgood ignored him and levered up to a sitting position. "How long have I been out?" he asked.

"Only a few minutes."

Osgood stared hard into the dark, as if they could see something there apart from the cold, black emptiness of the newly created tunnel. "I saw it again . . ." he said.

"Saw what?"

"Saw . . ." Osgood shook his head to clear away the thought. "Never mind. Have you checked for tiranium?"

The first assistant reached into his belt pack and took out a miniaturized Geiger counter. He turned it on and scanned the darkness as a flat humming noise indicated there was nothing there but useless rock.

Osgood didn't need to be told. "Then we'll never find it!" he bellowed and grappled to his feet. "Come on. We're going back up."

Michelle Osgood lay quietly in bed, looking at the pale light that diffused through the walls of the hospital treatment room. It was supposed to be soothing, carefully tested for a psychologically relaxing effect. Yearning for bright light and excitement, she found it depressing and dull. It was terribly boring to die slowly.

Helena could almost read her pretty young patient's thoughts as she packed up a set of instruments from the table at the foot of the bed. "We'll be testing a new heart for you this afternoon," she said, encouragingly. "There's always hope."

"Of course, Doctor," Michelle responded without enthusiasm.

It was somewhat pleasing for Helena to see the new light of interest that came into the girl's face as the deep, resonant voice of her husband sounded from the other side of the door. He was asking the duty nurse if he could see his wife. Helena felt that Michelle's happiness in seeing him was one of the few things that kept her going. But every time she saw Osgood, herself, she became more concerned about the stability of *his* mind.

He came through the door into the room like a great, brooding presence. Helena stepped in front of him, intercepting his intense, smouldering stare. She intended to warn him to be careful, not to upset his wife in any way, but he spoke first.

"Doctor, I want to be alone with my wife."

Then Helena noted with alarm that his face was purple along one side with bruising and that blood had matted into the beard on his chin. She reached up questioningly.

"It's nothing . . . a small cave-in. Leave us, please."

Helena decided the least trouble would be caused if she did as he asked, and she was also short of time to get the new heart ready for testing. Osgood waited till she had left before going over and bending down to his wife. He calmed her concern about his bruises, even forcing his sore lips apart in a loving smile.

"Michelle," he said with sudden seriousness, "you must listen to me. I have seen . . ." His eyes lifted up seeking something in the empty air. "I have seen a revelation. I have seen the future for us all."

"Patrick?" Michelle was bewildered by his change of mood.

"I've seen a storm of fire . . . and Alpha Base destroyed." The pressure of his hands on her arms stopped her from shaking her head. "Yes, I *have*. Only *we* can be saved. If you can have the faith . . . if you can believe in me," Patrick's voice vibrated with power, "I can save you!"

She didn't know if she were answering the call to faith or just her own cry of love as she reached up to him and said desperately, "Yes, Patrick, yes!"

The scene in the Command Center was unprecedented. The usual snappy and precise routine was gone. The neatness of uniform dress that was quite simple to maintain, thanks to the functional simplicity of suit design, was gone. Personnel leaned tiredly over their equipment, eyes drooping and listless. A trip from one side of the room to another seemed like a hike across a desert. Most of the men had discarded their jackets, and however possible, garments that had to be kept on were unfastened, hanging loosely and sodden with perspiration.

John Koenig, in spite of the heavy, unrelenting heat, felt a deep sense of urgency. The onset of the high temperature was a mystery, beginning and quickly escalating without any prior warning. The lower levels of the base were still relatively cool, but the Command Center was suffering worst.

Koenig looked around as Maya tiredly read out the latest statistical check to him. "Surface temperature now forty degrees centigrade and rising rapidly."

"Have we got any further in pinpointing a source?" he asked.

Maya shook her head. "It's out front somewhere, Commander. That's as specific as we can get . . . the computer print-outs . . ."

Koenig lost track of her words. The whole situation aggravated him intensely. It was the worst possible time for something like this to happen, with the base increasingly vulnerable because of dropping tiranium stocks. There were only a couple of weeks left until the critical point would be reached.

On top of that, he was privately worried about Helena. She had been in a miserable state when he came back from the Blue Zone mission . . . failing to see how much she had done for the Archanon boy, Etrec, and thinking instead only of the death of his father. She blamed herself for it, not seeing that the boy could only have been saved that way. Now she was overworking herself again . . . trying desperately to save the life of that young Osgood woman. He knew that if she didn't slow she would be needing treatment herself.

"I don't need computer print-outs to tell me it's hot and getting hotter!" Koenig suddenly exploded to his feet, silencing the room. "I need specifics! I need to know why and where this heat is coming from."

Calmly, Maya replied, "When the facts fail us, Commander, we must guess."

"Then get new facts!" Koenig turned to face his second in command. "Tony, can you squeeze any more power out of the air-conditioning system?"

Verdeschi shook his head curtly. "It's already on overload . . . practically combustible."

"Then *what* do you recommend?"

Tony smiled and gave an impish sidelong look at Maya. "Well, I'd say . . . let's relax uniform regulations completely. We should all get as comfortable as we can."

Koenig couldn't help smiling at the impertinence of the suggestion, but also noted that it had its practical side. He looked over his shoulder and saw Bill Fraser, the crack Eagle pilot, listening with interest.

"What would you suggest, Bill?" he asked.

"Me? Hmm . . . well, I don't see how you can find an answer without going and looking for it. But then, I think like a pilot."

"Maybe that's not a bad way to think," Koenig said with a smile. "Let's you and I take a ride in an Eagle."

Helena studied the pumping valves of the artificial heart with frantic concentration. The test fluids moved through its plastic tube arteries with bubbling alacrity. Yet she could tell from the computer test that simulated Michelle Osgood's life functions that the heart was just not functioning with enough precise efficiency to keep her alive. The computer indicated that she was "dying" from the man-made heart's malfunctioning. If Helena took out Michelle's own ailing heart and replaced it with this one, she really would die.

Helena turned away from the test rig and looked back at her written analysis. There had to be a simple answer from applied science. Tapping the keyboard of her console, she called up a visual image of Victor Bergman's artificial heart. The film clip of the X-ray showed it beating normally inside Victor's heart . . . such a long time ago since he died. She thought that he might well have lived forever if it had not been for a fateful accident.

The slide changed to a thermographic photograph of Bergman's heart, the heat pattern making a healthy display of colors. She asked for it to be replaced with her own latest attempt, the tenth, and could clearly see the contrast where the heart valves appeared lifelessly pale. The one main weakness—the one specific advantage Bergman's heart had over any she could devise. Victor's heart had a coat of tiranium over the valves. Unfortunately, all the tiranium in stock on Alpha at present was needed to keep the life support systems of the Moon Base going for as long as possible.

And so far she hadn't found an acceptable substitute. She looked at the test tube that Doctor Vincent had brought in for her. It contained a silicone derivative that just might be the answer they had been looking for. She decided to apply it to the heart valves and get a computer opinion right away. There was no point in wasting time on a blood flow test until the more crucial doubt was settled.

She looked around sharply as Doctor Vincent came into the room, followed by the massive form of Patrick Osgood. He looked around the laboratory from under his shaggy brows with obvious disdain.

Helena tried to ignore his presence, handing Doctor Vincent the checklist for the test. Meanwhile she dealt with applying the silicone to the valves as Osgood watched from a certain distance . . . as if he thought he might be infected by too close a contact with the heresies of science.

"We're ready to test," Doctor Vincent said.

Osgood snorted. "Ah. I've come at the right time to witness your success."

Helena tried to ignore the sarcasm. "We *are* trying."

"Obviously. It's just that I have a different faith than yours." Osgood's face and voice grew dark like gathering storm clouds. "I have a more certain knowledge of what is to be. *And* what is not to be."

A chill of premonition passed through Helena. She shrugged it off and returned to preparing for the test.

The dials flickered to life as the mechanical circulatory system began to pulse. The silvery heart began to beat with a regular and strong rhythm. The monitor beeped a steady electronic echo, and after a moment Helena's hopes began to rise.

This time the computer feedback on the heart function was to simulate life, so that when the system failure came, the entire mechanism sputtered to a halt. Helena's hope evaporated as the heart "died" in its case . . . another failure.

"Hmmmph!" sneered Osgood. "So much for blasphemy. Did you think that scientists could give the gift of life?"

"We're Michelle's only hope!" Helena shouted. She turned away to calm herself, trying to bear in mind that Osgood would be feeling the strain of his wife's illness more than she would.

"All right, Ben," she said to Doctor Vincent, "back to the drawing board."

"Again?"

"Again! And again . . . until we succeed!"

Koenig and Frazer took the Eagle on a long sweeping zigzag across the path of the Moon, searching . . . seeking . . . any answer at all. They could see or detect nothing except the steady flow of heat which swept past them and on down to the face of Luna. At least the Eagle's air conditioning was designed to keep the craft's occupants comfortable in higher temperatures than Moon Base . . . plus an extra insulation against atmosphere reentry temperatures.

It was a reasonably comfortable Commander Koenig who radioed back to the Command Center for the latest information. "Any new facts, new readings . . . new anything, Maya?"

When Maya came on the screen, Koenig was surprised to see that she was attractively attired in a revealing halter-style top. "Nothing, Commander. The temperature just keeps rising."

"How about tempers?" He remembered with discomfort his own irritable outburst.

"No tantrums yet. Have you discovered any new information?"

Koenig shook his head as Verdeschi cut into the communication. "Commander, I think we had better prepare to move all the nonessential personnel to the lower tunnels if the temperature doesn't level off in the next few hours. At its present rate of rise we should just about be starting to cook in here by then."

"Agreed, Tony. Arrange it as you see fit in my absence . . ."

Seeing that Koenig was about to sign off, Helena quickly cut into the communication from her desk in the Medical Center where she had been listening.

"John," she said imploringly, "I have a special request. We've got a life or death medical problem, and I need your authorization."

Koenig frowned in bafflement.

"It's Michelle Osgood," Helena continued. "I need your approval to release some tiranium . . . just a few grains. It is absolutely essential if I'm going to perfect an artificial heart for her."

Everyone who was litening in to the exchange started at the request. It was only too evident the difficulty of the decision that Koenig faced.

"A few grains are absolutely essential for our life support system on Alpha, Helena. We're using up an extra quantity during this emergency . . . and so far it seems that our stocks are irreplaceable!"

Sadly, Helena replied, "So is Michelle Osgood's life."

There was a long silence, a hissing of white sound as Koenig debated his decision with himself. "In normal conditions I would take the risk . . . but . . . I'm sorry. It's one life against hundreds. I can't jeopardize all of Alpha. If there's any other way, I know you'll find it."

Helena couldn't hide her disappointment. She understood perfectly the logic of Koenig's decision, but saving Michelle's life had come to mean such a great deal to her.

"I wish you luck, Helena," Koenig said at last. "Eagle One, out."

Verdeschi had called together several of the leaders of the Moon Base's mining teams. They stood attentively in the corridor as Tony held up in front of him an eyedropper full of clear liquid. From the end of the dropper a small glistening bubble expanded as he gently depressed the rubber bulb. When the weight of the tiny tear was sufficient, it came free of the dropper's end and fell to the floor. There was a nerve-shattering bang and a searing flash of light.

Tony retained his calmness very steadfastly as he laid the eyedropper down on a cushioned table. Then he turned back to the anxious miners.

"As you all know, gentlemen . . . as it is your professional interest to know . . . hypernitro becomes unstable at around fifty degrees centigrade. As you have just seen from the demonstration, the temperature inside Alpha is rapidly approaching that point."

One of the miners, a grizzled old hand, completed the line of thought for all of them. "And we've got a ton of the stuff in our storeroom."

Tony nodded. "We've got to get the lot of it out of storage and take it down to the deep levels. And we've got less than an hour to do it."

They all moved off together to a travel tube and found Maya waiting there for them. She opened the door for them with her comlock and also showed Tony that she had brought with her the safety sensor he had requested. Its very mild sonar effect would enable them to evaluate just how molecularly torpid each container of hypernitro was before they tried to move it.

The storage area in the engineers' section was garishly signposted for danger for several hundred yards before they arrived at the actual Explosives Storeroom. The built-in warning system over the door was already flashing a Yellow Alert before they arrived. Tony tried to reassure himself with the knowledge that it was triggered by a much higher safety margin than was really necessary.

"All right . . . everybody," he said in almost a whisper as the executive authority of his comlock opened the maximum security door, "breathe easy and walk lightly. Bring the trolleys out slowly and one at a time."

Holding the accurately keyed sensor she had brought in front of her, Maya slid gracefully into the room.

"How is it?" Tony asked as the crew got carefully to work.

"It's fine," she said, "just as long as nobody sneezes."

The work went smoothly enough so that half the trolleys were soon out and on their way down below in the lift. Tony kept a watch on the upward-creeping mercury in the thermometer on the wall. It was only at 47 degrees centigrade but the room's own automatic warning had moved into Red Alert and was flashing like a hysterical lighthouse.

It was a heart-jerking surprise when Patrick Osgood suddenly strode into the storeroom and grasped Tony by the arm in a vice-like grip.

"Patrick!"

Osgood growled, "I want a word with you, Tony."

Several of the miners in the room had frozen at what they were doing, feeling that even the rough voice of the big man might cause the delicate explosive to shake. Verdeschi smiled with casual friendliness.

"Sure, Pat," he said, "only take it easy. It's a little touch-and-go around here right now. What do you say we go for a little walk and be private?"

"Right here . . . right now!" Osgood thundered.

Feeling the painful bands of Osgood's fingers closing on his arm, Tony still managed to keep on smiling. "Listen," he said gently, "I'm sorry about Michelle. If only we'd found some more tiranium . . ."

"But we didn't find it." Osgood was curt.

"Don't give up hope."

"I haven't. I'm just not going to waste any more time waiting for the misguided fools who call themselves 'scientists' and 'doctors'. I have had good news. There will be salvation for my wife."

"How?" Tony asked carefully.

"*I* am her salvation. I have supreme knowledge. Only faith can triumph over death . . . only faith can give life."

105

"Yeah, that's interesting, Pat." Tony was too aware that valuable seconds were ticking past and they still had a lot of hypernitro to move. "But if you can just excuse me right now..."

Osgood shook Tony forcibly, so that his teeth chattered together. "Go ahead, mock me, Tony. Just because you haven't the power of faith that I have..."

Suddenly Tony felt genuinely upset and looked it. Even in the midst of his duty and serious responsibility, he could recall that Patrick Osgood was one of his oldest friends.

"Mock you? C'mon, Pat, I was the best man at your wedding, remember?"

"Yes, I remember. And it saddens me to know that I will see you die. But at least you will die honorably with the rest... and not flee in disgrace like the Commander."

Verdeschi shook his head, feeling that Osgood's ravings were getting progressively more bizarre. "Pat, I know what you're going through over Michelle. I know how much it hurts, but believe me, no one is running away. The Commander just went out on a long-range reconnaissance to find out what's causing the temperature build-up."

"I already have the answer. I had a true vision... I've seen the holocaust. Moon Base Alpha will be consumed by flames."

Tony knew he had to get Osgood out of the room. He laid his free arm over the wide shoulders and edged toward the door.

"There are all sorts of visions, Pat," Tony said with persuasive kindness. "Why don't we go see Doctor Russell and find out..."

Osgood shrugged off the arm violently. "You think I'm going strange... you think I'm mad just because I can see the future... because I say Alpha will be destroyed. Well, it will... but not Michelle. I'm getting her and taking her with me!"

Verdeschi reached for Osgood again, and this time the big man lifted him up and flung him backwards.

Tony crashed into a trolley loaded with hypernitro and just managed to steady it from falling over while two more crewmen threw themselves at Osgood.

With a mighty roar he smashed one of them down with a punch to the face. The other man slung his arms around the bull-like neck and was lifted off his feet.

Tony leaped back to the fray, striving to pin Osgood's arms before he knocked against the carefully balanced cannisters of explosive. Osgood bellowed again and slung him away. The third man followed, flying head first into a storage rack.

Maya stifled a scream as the warning tone on her sensor shrilled stridently, a warning that the fluid was on the verge of detonation. Tony scrambled desperately toward Osgood, but he was stunned by the handling he had received so far and found himself trapped in a bear hug.

The strength in the circling arms doubled with insanity and the force cut grimly across Tony's ribs and spine. He looked up to Patrick's face to appeal to him to stop ... but the eyes were vacant ... the brain behind them seeing only its own apocalyptic visions. Tony couldn't breathe, and red stars began to flare in his brain as the grip tightened even more.

It was almost like a hallucination when a savage yowl sounded behind him and a heavy, hot breath passed by his ear. He had never before in his life seen anything like the scaly, long-bodied beast that had locked itself into Osgood's shoulder muscle with a trap-like set of teeth. Its plates gleamed with blue light and red, multi-faceted eyes waved on the end of furry stalks.

With a bellow of pain and abhorrence, Osgood let Tony drop to the floor and pushed the thing away from him. As it reeled back, he turned and ran out, blood gushing from the deep bite wound.

Tony took a gasping breath and stared at the vile, alien creature. He wondered if he, too, were having some kind of vision. Then the air around the thing became charged with energy and a translucent field made it disappear from view. Out of the shimmering ripples stepped Maya, re-transformed to her own beautiful self.

She stooped quickly down to Tony, desperate to know how badly Osgood had hurt him. He smiled to show her that he was recovering.

"Thanks," he said. "I'm glad you got him off me, but you nearly gave me heart failure. I won't ask you what it was you turned into ... it would only keep me from forgetting it in a hurry."

Maya kissed him lightly on the cheek and moved over to see how badly hurt the other men were. Tony pulled out his comlock and called through to the Security Section. Osgood had to be found. He was a danger to them all, wandering around in his state of mind ... especially at a time like this.

CHAPTER TEN

Velma Hill was an excellent secretary and laboratory assistant, but she was also nervous. She needed a great deal of reassurance from Tony Verdeschi before she could be convinced it was now safe to go over to the Explosives Storeroom. She had been instructed to take an inventory of the other explosives that were in stock ... all of which were quite safe unless specifically detonated by mechanical or electrical means.

She stepped out of the travel tube to the very appreciative glances of two junior engineers. For the sake of comfort she was dressed in a bikini, and its black shape moulded around her tan skin in delicious harmony. She walked on down the corridor in a pertly pleased stride, her ego glowing. As far as she was concerned, the heat wave could last forever.

Only when she came in sight of the Explosives Storeroom door did she slow down. She just couldn't get over her phobia of things that made loud noises. She unclipped her comlock from the side elastic of her bikini pants and prepared to unlock the door. Then she noticed that it was already standing ajar.

She hadn't expected anyone else to be there but presumed that it must be one of the mining team leaders. They were the only other Alpha staff members who were authorized entry. Intrigued to see who it was, and prepared to receive another homage of interested ogling, she stepped inside.

With a shrill scream she froze just inside the door. Across the room Patrick Osgood faced her, his arm hanging down and coated with blood. His face was pallid and damp with sweat from some great strain.

He tried to shuffle toward her, mumbling inaudibly for her to be quiet, but the effort was too much. He plunged forward and collapsed senselessly on the floor.

"Security!" Velma shouted into her comlock, voice fraught with terror. "Security, come in, please!"

Verdeschi stayed beside the stretcher all the way to the Medical Section. Osgood never quite came fully awake, but tossed restlessly, his head shaking from side to side. He kept mumbling about fire from the sky and called out his wife's name.

A security guard kept an eye on Osgood in the emergency reception while Tony went through to the research area. Helena and Doctor Vincent were hard at work, as he had expected them to be. Diagrams and formulas relating to the construction of artificial organs were scattered everywhere, along with empty coffee cups and sandwich wrappers.

Helena looked up with fatigued eyes and took a moment to focus and recognize who had come.

"Helena," Tony said urgently, "we've got Osgood. He's in emergency."

Helena and Ben followed Tony back to the feverish

man. His eyes were open when they got there, and he watched them with steely hostility when they came close.

"How is he?" Tony asked after Helena had checked Osgood over with the bioscope.

"He's lost a lot of blood." She turned to Doctor Vincent. "Ben, wheel the surgical lamp and instrument table closer, please."

Osgood strained to sit up. "When the fire comes, flee to the catacombs!"

"The what?" asked Ben.

"The tunnels . . . the tunnels," Osgood ranted. "You'll be safe there."

"There is no fire, Patrick," Tony said soothingly.

"It is coming!" Osgood shouted and struggled again to move off the stretcher.

Helena held him firmly back and reached out for the bottle of antiseptic. She was anxious to clean up the wound and see just how much damage had been done. The penetration looked as though it might have gone right down to the bone.

Osgood seemed to calm momentarily. He kept still, then spoke in a very slow and sensible manner. "Doctor Russell. If you look closely under my coat . . . you'll see I've wire myself with several packs of explosive. I have made myself a human bomb."

There was a sudden deathly silence, and Helena's hands stopped still over Osgood's chest.

"Patrick," chastised Tony, "this is no time for games."

Helena shook her head to warn him. "May I examine you?" she asked Osgood.

"Yes, but very carefully. Everyone else stay away."

Helena cut away the sleeve of the tunic first to check on the wound. Osgood was still losing blood profusely, but it didn't look as though the bone had been damaged. She wiped the edges of the wound clean and stuck on some temporary sutures. Only then did she lift up the garment over the big heaving chest and look underneath. She could just see a thick vest of very expertly connected explosive charges.

"He's telling the truth," Helena told Tony. "It looks

like he could blow up the entire hospital if he set himself off."

"He wouldn't do that," Tony protested.

Helena's frown reminded Tony that Osgood was not in his right mind. She said, "He just might, though. Personally I'm more worried right now about saving his arm than I am about explosives. Patrick, you've got to let me operate . . ."

This time Osgood managed to push himself up and swing his legs off the stretcher. "I will let you quickly bandage my arm. But then you will take me to my wife."

"This wound needs extensive attention . . . you could do with a transfusion—"

Osgood stopped Helena's protests by simply raising his good hand. In it he held an electrical clip. The conducting teeth were open, held apart by the pressure of Osgood's hand on the plastic handles. "I don't want any arguments, just a quick bandage . . . and then I'm going."

Quietly, resentfully, Helena took the gauze pad and began to apply it over the injury. Tony and Ben stood well back, studying the grim determination on Osgood's face.

Osgood had trouble walking, but he managed it. Tony still wondered if he really would set off an explosion that would claim so many innocent lives. Somehow there seemed a greater risk that he would stumble and cause a catastrophe by accident. Still, it was a bluff they couldn't risk calling. They had to cooperate.

Michelle Osgood was under mild sedation when they got to her room, but Patrick's pleading voice was enough to rouse her. Helena argued and implored as he helped her from the bed.

"Michelle is mine, not yours!" Osgood shouted.

"She's not yours to kill," Helena insisted. "Only a new heart will save her life . . . and we're building a new one right now. She'll never survive if you take her away."

"How many hearts have you tried already?" Osgood challenged with a cynical sneer. "Your medicine is useless. Now I will show you how my faith can *really* save life."

111

Helena wouldn't give in . . . she *couldn't* give in. "If I only had some tiranium, I guarantee I could make a heart that worked. I will get some, Patrick. As soon as I can talk to John, I'll make him understand how much it means and he'll release enough for me to use."

Osgood didn't feel like wasting any more time on conversation. He curled his arm around Michelle's waist, the hand with the trigger mechanism resting on her hip. With loving care he guided her toward the door, and the others moved out of his path.

"It's a long way, Michelle, but we're going together," they heard him whisper as they moved past.

Michelle was unsteady but kept walking. "I love you," she said, just as the door closed behind them.

CHAPTER ELEVEN

Even though they could still see nothing on the screen, Koenig could at least now understand why. They were moving through a vast plasma cloud. One moment they had been in the limitless darkness of empty night; then, without warning, they were inside the cloud. It was still darkness, but this time it was because the external sensors were muffled. Nothing in the audio-visual wavelengths of the spectrum could get through.

"Well, Commander," observed Frazer, "now we know why we *didn't* know. The question is, exactly what's on the other side of this cloud?"

"There're only two ways to find that out, Bill," Koenig said dryly. "We can go back to Alpha and wait for whatever it is to come through to us ... or we can go on through in the Eagle and see in advance. But then we'll have to hope we can still get back with the information."

Frazer grunted and settled back deeper in his seat as he made the ship accelerate forward. "We'll get back, Commander."

Along the line of their travel the plasma cloud was less thick than it was deep, so very suddenly they shot out the other side into empty space. At least it registered as empty on all the monitors, but according to the picture on the screens they could have just as likely plunged into the heart of a cool orange sun. The deep, ominous color was all around them, a bright ocherous hue that swirled with flares of combustion.

"Look! There!" yelled Koenig. "There's our heat wave."

Far out ahead of them they could see the cause of the light. The orange sky was simply an illusion aided by the plasma cloud. In fact, the light was a weak advance projection of a wave of twisting, licking, and snaking hydrogen fire that stretched across thousands of miles of space. It was a fire storm; the first they had ever seen so grimly near. And it was getting closer every second.

"We're going to have to outrun it and warn Alpha. What's the estimated speed of the thing?" Koenig asked.

Frazer coded the question for the Eagle's computer, and the answering digits popped up on the screen for them both to see. "Hmm," Koenig said, doing a quick calculation of his own. "Just under two hours until Alpha and the storm cross paths. Let's get back through this cloud and let them know."

The gap between the Eagle and the storm had narrowed dramatically even in the moments they had been speaking. Deceptive tentacles raced out far ahead of the inferno's main body and would soon be slashing at the Eagle if they didn't move quickly. Frazer threw the ship into a banked hairpin turn, diving back into the cloud and picking up speed every second.

They came belting out the other side at maximum

thrust, and as soon as the transmitters snapped back on, Koenig was signalling top priority to the Moon Base.

"This is Eagle One to Moon Base Alpha," he announced. "Code, Red Alert. I repeat, Red Alert!"

As the Eagle dived for home Koenig clicked the buttons under his screen to have a look at the rear view with the camera mounted on the craft's roof. A long tuber of scarlet heat was already through the cloud, slithering out like a fast-growing devil's weed.

Fraser had identified Verdeschi and gave him the official facts. "Hydrogen fire storm moving toward fifteen-degree diagonal collision with Alpha Moon Base. Estimated time of arrival, eleven hundred hours. Computer estimates on lunar surface area to be affected, fifty miles width across full Moon face. Impact variables between one and five megatons." For the last segment of information, Fraser dropped the cool, official jargon. "And man, is it going to get hot!"

Koenig cut in. "Tony, activate the plan to move to the lower levels right away. We hope to get back just before the storm hits, so don't lock the door on us."

"Right, Commander," acknowledged Tony. "We'll leave a key under the mat."

"Say, Tony," Fraser said, "how about having a nice cool beer waiting for us when we get back? Never mind the scale of one to ten ... just brew up your usual suds and put it on ice."

Tony tried hard not to take offence at the slur on his brewing talents. Then he reckoned that he'd have the last laugh, anyway, since there wasn't sufficient refrigeration left in Alpha to make an ice cube at the high heat levels.

"Is Helena there, Tony?" Koenig asked. In fact, she was standing by, waiting for a chance to speak. Ready to plead the case for Michelle's heart for all she was worth ... and to tell Koenig what had happened to the Osgoods. With this new information about the approaching danger to the Moon Base, she imagined her task would be harder than ever.

"I'm here, John," she said.

"Helena, we can't predict how well the base will come through this storm. We may all get blown to hell. But I think you can help yourself to a little tiranium to make a new heart for that young lady . . . if there's still time."

Helena could only nod, her eyes welling with tears. The screen went blank as the Eagle cut off communication. They had enough to think about then, just getting back to the base.

Tony moved purposefully over to the control panel, seeing with comfort that the rest of the center staff were already initiating emergency procedures. He placed his hand over the red button and pressed it down. Instantly the entire complex shivered with the sound of the Red Alert klaxons going off.

To the general hubbub was added the echo of the intercom system, instructions being passed on to the fire-fighting crew, the engineers, and the hospital staff. Tony dialled himself through to the power plant. "I want all nonessential machinery and equipment shut down . . . right now! And I mean *all.*"

Looking around he could see Helena waiting anxiously for a chance to speak to him. He could guess what she wanted.

"Go on, Helena," he said quickly. "I believe you've got an important job to do. I think your medical crew can handle all the evacuation routine without you."

Helena smiled gratefully and rushed out to collect the small amount of tiranium she would require and to get it safely back to the lab. The new prosthetic heart was already assembled . . . all she had to do was coat the valves and then they could test it.

When Maya had finished putting the instruction for the nature of the emergency status into the computer, she looked up and saw Tony's friendly smile.

"Well, you lovely Psychon witch," he said, "it looks like it's up to you and me to find Patrick. We've got about half an hour before they'll have to start moving people below. We've got to make sure he isn't waiting down there to blow us all up when we arrive."

Maya signalled her understanding with a quick lift

of the chin. "Tony," she wondered fleetingly, "do you think he really did have a vision?"

Verdeschi couldn't answer her. All he knew was that when he looked up to the big screen now he could make out a far-away wave of barbed fire. It had come through the plasma cloud and was getting quickly bigger. The next destination on its route was Alpha.

Deep in the blackness of the catacombs, Patrick and Michelle were resting, and Patrick could see a fire of his own. It rippled in the dark, destroying Alpha Moon Base and all the non-believing fools inside it. The faithless would perish, and only he and Michelle would survive. He could even see the bed . . . the brass bed of conjugal bliss sitting innocently on the Moon sands. A ball of flame crashed into it, but Osgood smiled with knowing triumph. The flame could not claim the life of Michelle. He could feel her sitting on the cave floor . . . just beside him. Her breath panted with weariness, and her failing heart fluttering under his touch . . . but she would live. They had beaten the fire together, and now his faith would support and revive her.

"Don't be afraid," he said comfortably to her.

"I'm not afraid when I'm with you. I know you love me." Her voice caught with hesitation. "But . . . but, Patrick, wasn't there any hope for me at the hospital?"

"None at all," he answered adamantly.

"Doctor Russell tried very hard."

Patrick caressed the fine silk of his wife's hair. "She failed utterly. But *I* will not. Can you walk now?"

"Just another minute. Perhaps you could sing for me . . . the way you used to."

In the darkness, Osgood's deep, vibrant voice began softly to intone a beautiful and haunting Gregorian chant. He let the song grow in volume until it resounded through the very fiber of the cave walls. Michelle sighed and relaxed even more against him, feeling enormously comforted by the sound. Her eyes were closed, so she didn't see, as Patrick did, the distant glimmer of a torch beam. It shook as the person carrying it walked toward them.

Patrick ceased his singing and said with easy firmness, "And now we really must go."

"Thank you, Patrick," she whispered. "Yes, I will try now."

Osgood rushed her as much as he could, but even he could sense the limit of her resources. He only wished he had two good arms so he could carry her. Anxiously he looked back and could see the search was rapidly gaining on them. His belief that they had found their salvation and were safe had been shattered; they were still threatened with being dragged back up to die with the rest of the fools. He knew, however, he could and *would* blow them all to bits rather than give in.

The tunnel curved and twisted, so he managed to keep them out of the beam of the light. Whoever it was was relentless, however, and he could tell by occasional snatches of voice that they were still catching up. He couldn't risk using his own torch, but moved through the catacombs with a long refined miner's instinct. But, after five minutes of a steady pace, Michelle's legs collapsed under her.

"I haven't any more strength," she protested.

He tried to lift her up. "We're almost safe now ... please, just a little farther."

"No ... no, I must rest."

Osgood looked frantically back to see if their pursuers had come into view. "You *must* go on!" he pleaded.

Michelle only slumped down further, momentarily blacking out. Osgood stretched himself out beside her and realized that loss of blood and tension were taking their toll of his strength as well.

"Can you hear me?" he whispered in her ear.

Michelle responded to the beloved voice, saying, "Don't worry, Patrick. I'm not afraid to die."

The sentence brought a new surge of power to Patrick. He could not bear to hear her talk of dying—it shook him right down to his soul. "You will never die!" he said. "I will not let you go. You are being and breath ... and you will never be destroyed! Trust me ... trust me."

They were still fifty yards away when Verdeschi's light caught the two bodies lying side by side on the tunnel floor. Tony felt sure that Michelle must be finished by then and that Osgood was probably in pretty bad shape himself.

Maya's vision was keener, however, and she detected movement from both the people they were seeking. "There. There, look!"

Patrick Osgood powered himself up to his feet, swaying but with teeth gritted to continue the chase. He reached down his hand, and unbelievably, Michelle rose up from the ground, her face beaming at his. Together they walked swiftly and smoothly away, out of sight around another twist in the labyrinth.

Tony and Maya, with two security guards right behind, hurried after them. They had just about reached the point where they had seen the Osgoods lying when Tony's comlock buzzed for his attention.

"Verdeschi," he spoke into it, still moving forward.

He recognized Helena's voice. "Tony, we've just run a complete range of tests . . ." she could hardly contain her excitement, "and it's working! It's working perfectly. You've got to find her and bring her back."

"All right, Helena," he replied. "We've almost caught up with them . . ."

Suddenly the entire Moon rumbled with the sound of a mighty explosion. The floor underfoot swayed, and there was a deep roll like kettle drums. Tony looked up and saw dust and rock chips floating from the tunnel ceiling.

"Tony," questioned Helena, "what was that?"

"I think it must be the advance wave of the fire storm. It's going to be a rough ride from now on."

Desperately, Helena urged, "You must get her, Tony. We can't lose her now!"

"We'll get her," he said with firm reassurance. He only wished he felt as confident as he sounded, bracing himself against the wall as he heard another shock wave racing toward them.

CHAPTER TWELVE

When Fraser brought the Eagle down toward the Moon surface in a landing pattern, they could see that the streamers of fire that had whipped past them in space had already caused some damage to the aboveground Moon Base. Several buildings were on fire, but all of them had been vacated by the move underground months before.

As they scanned the terrain for further signs of destruction they caught sight of a fairly large fireball striking the rim of a crater about five miles away. In a perfect imitation of eruption the cavity gushed with flame and the smoke of scattered dust. Fraser estimated that the force of it would have been enough to knock a man off his feet right on the other side of Luna.

Koenig called down to the Command Center to check on the situation and to clear their landing.

"Sahn here, Commander," answered the Senior Operations Supervisor.

"We're making our landing approach, Sahn. Is the flight deck still all right?"

Sahn grinned into the monitor. "Affirmative, Commander. We're ready for you. As soon as you touch down, I'll get the travel tube on the airlock. I don't recommend that you hang around for a post-flight instrument check . . . get inside and underground as fast as you can. The main body of the fire storm will be hitting us very soon."

"Right, Sahn. What's the situation so far?"

The man's usually imperturbable face became just a little uneasy. "There's a lot of topside damage, sir, but we're not suffering much down here. A few minor casualties so far, but nothing serious. The evacuation to the lower tunnels is under way, but we're being slowed down by Mister Verdeschi's orders not to use bottom level until he says it's all right."

"Where is Tony now?" Koenig asked, puzzled by the situation.

"He's down there, sir, bottom tunnel. I think he's looking for someone."

Koenig looked anxiously across at Fraser, who was equally bewildered. Settling himself better in the contour seat, he pointed toward the floor. "Come on, Bill. Get me down there so I can find out what the hell is going on."

The rumble and shake of the stone all around them had become so regular and expected that Tony was managing to walk even as it occurred. It was just like a sailor getting his sea legs and anticipating the roll of a ship's deck. He couldn't get used to the dust that the jolts were shaking loose, however, and both he and the security men were troubled with coughing. Maya didn't mind it so much, but her Psychon lungs had a more efficient filtering method in their respiration system than theirs.

Several times they had caught sight of the Osgoods in the torch beam, but the couple moved as though they had got a new burst of energy and they were having trouble closing the gap.

Tony stopped for a moment to wipe the sweat off his face. If he left it too long, the dust would cake around his eyes like a mud mask.

"Isn't it strange," Maya said, "how close to the truth Osgood's prophecy was? I suppose we should feel comforted to know we're following a prophet at a time when the face of the Moon is being blown up."

Tony sighed. "Sure, unless *he* blows up."

"Yes. There is still that to worry about, even if we catch them."

Tony started to move ahead. "We must catch them soon. They *must* be exhausted by now."

Maya caught his arm. "Wait. I have an idea. Turn off your torch."

Tony was willing to try anything that brought a quick conclusion to the pursuit and the safe delivery of Michelle to the Medical Center. He did as Maya requested and sensed, even without being able to see through the pitch blackness, that she was undergoing a transformation. Seconds later, an oddly shaped and velvety hand with only three fingers slipped into his.

"One of you get hold of the back of my jacket," Tony told the security men, "and the other get hold of his."

Linked together they moved off at a steady jog. Whatever form Maya had adopted, Tony guessed it must have some kind of bat-like radar to find its way accurately without light. He just hoped it wasn't as horrific looking as the thing in the Explosives Storeroom had been.

They ran on for quite a few minutes, gaining constantly on Osgood. He had slowed his pace as soon as he could no longer see the torch beam. The sound of feet running after him would have been undetectable in the rumble and thump of seismic waves racing down from the surface.

Abruptly Maya stopped and, as Tony waited uncertainly, the fur-covered appendage let him go. A peculiar purring sound hissed near his ear, words that seemed to say, "Wait . . . till . . . ten . . . then . . . light."

As Maya left him he raised his torch, aiming it straight ahead of him down the tunnel. Silently he counted to ten and then pressed the button with his thumb.

Michelle Osgood was sitting on the ground, her back against a large boulder and her head slumped down. Patrick stared into the stark light, dazzled and astonished.

"Pat!" Tony shouted, "It's me . . . Tony. I want to talk to you. I've got good news from Helena!"

Osgood shook his head with anger, probably not even comprehending the words. He raised his right hand with the plastic clip in it, the copper jaws coming closer and closer together. As soon as they touched, the circuit from the battery he had in one pocket would be complete. The current would flow through and into the charges he had strapped to his body. Their six bodies, what was left of them, would probably never be found.

With a terrifying roar, something sprang into the area of the light. A coat of black and red stripes shivered all over its upright body and curved, razor-sharp claws slid cat-like from its paws. The head was nothing more than a thick, gray membrane . . . low on the shoulders and with a puckered large gap for a mouth.

Osgood was stunned rigid by the vision, something Maya must have been counting on. His hand was halfway open, and Maya bounded the rest of the distance between them before the fingers could twitch a fraction more. She did not attack him this time, however, but lashed out with a claw and accurately sliced through the dangling wires leading to the battery. As Osgood's mind spun back into action, he let the clip go and it clicked harmlessly shut.

"Noooo!" he howled with disappointment. He was crushed by this final defeat and turned and ran headlong down the tunnel.

For the moment, Tony was more concerned with Michelle and moved quickly to her side to see if she was still alive. The answer was "barely," her breathing irregular and her heartbeat weak and fluttering.

"Get her up to the Med Center," he told the security men, still goggle-eyed at the creature Maya had transformed herself into. "Fast as you can, damnit!"

When they started off, he turned back to Maya. "I'm going after Patrick now," he said. "He may lose his will to live now that we've got Michelle. He could even rewire the explosives and blow himself—and me—to pieces. But I can't leave him." He left the question of whether she would help him unspoken.

Understanding, she drew back her alien claws and held out the soft black hand once again.

Koenig strode purposefully into the Medical Center and went straight across to the sealed viewing booth or the operating theater. Down below, under the filter-clarified floodlights, Helena was just completing the transplant operation and the surgery team were clearing up.

Through a speaker he heard Ben Vincent say, "Pressure improving . . . heart rate still irregular."

Helena looked up so that she could see the graph projections on the wall screen for herself. A nurse wiped the beads of sweat off her brows for her, and she returned to applying the sutures.

"Going on audio," Ben reported, and then the increasingly rhythmic ka-thumping was amplified for them all to hear. "Heart rate getting better."

Helena finished and stepped back, tugging off her plastic gloves. The nurse swabbed the closed incision and applied a dressing while the theater attendants readied the table to be wheeled out.

Frequently a loud crash could be heard through the insulated walls and the floor shuddered from another bolt hitting up above. The conditions would have made the operation terribly difficult to perform, Koenig thought, but he knew that the girl's condition must have been desperate for Helena to go ahead.

As Helena and Ben came through the doors to the sterilization room, Koenig walked around to join them.

"John!" Helena cried with delight at seeing him. It still didn't disguise the deep lines of tiredness around her eyes . . . but at least they sparkled at the success of the operation and at his return.

"How is she?" Koenig asked, then before Helena could answer, changed the question. "I know she's all right . . . how are you?"

Helena flushed with pleasure at his concern. "I'm fine . . . a little tired, is all."

"Well, now you can get some rest . . . on official orders. The worst of the storm has passed, and things will be quieting down." Koenig placed a fingertip in the corner of her smile. "You need a good night's sleep."

123

Helena shrugged and shook her head. "Not yet, John. There's still a problem."

Doctor Vincent led the way through to the post-operative care room. Michelle looked very much at peace, deeply sedated and resting on the white-sheeted bed. The instruments showed her vital signs were picking up nicely.

"She looks fine," Koenig said.

Frowning with doubt, Helena stared at the girl. "She's fine now, but what about when she wakes up and finds out her husband's missing . . . or that he's dead?" Helena looked as though she might suddenly cry, the stress taking its toll. "I can give her a new heart, but I can't give her the will to live. She'll need Patrick for that. I'm afraid all our work . . . all our hope may be for nothing."

An old familiar voice suddenly shouted out. "Sorry to tell you that you're wrong . . . but you're wrong!"

Turning around, they all saw with surprise the dirt-smeared face of Tony Verdeschi looking past the corner of the door. He wore a gleaming, lopsided Italian smile.

"Tony!" said Koenig.

"I'm not very clean, so I won't come in." Tony's smile got bigger. "I just thought you'd like to know I've got Patrick out here. He's not very fit, but he's alive."

Helena started to rush across the room, saying brightly, "And we're going to keep him that way."

Two days later, when the routine of the Moon Base was just about back to normal and both Osgoods were well on the road to recovery, Tony Verdeschi invited Maya, Helena, and Commander Koenig to join him for a celebration drink in his quarters. They all sat around expectantly while Tony's homebuilt brewing apparatus bubbled and glugged with yellow liquid.

Verdeschi looked hopeful with anticipation, but Maya was a picture of skepticism.

"Just look at the color," enthused Tony, "pure amber. Come on, Maya, that consistency is perfect . . . not a bubble in sight. I tell you, on a scale of one to ten, this will go right through the roof."

124

"Just so I don't when I drink it," Maya replied.

Tony drew off a measure of the liquid in a glass beaker and held it up to the light. He stretched it out for Helena's inspection.

"Looks pretty healthy, Tony," she laughed.

"Here's a toast to Mr. and Mrs. Patrick Osgood. May they live happily ever after. Now the first trial sip . . ."

Helena raised a hand of warning. "Are you sure this is really a good idea, Tony? Remember what our computer analysis said about your last brew?"

Tony blushed and showed his exasperation. "I know. I know. Unfit for human consumption. But what the heck does a computer know, anyway? No lust for adventure . . . no daring desire for experience."

Without another word he raised the glass and took a good mouthful of the fluid. He held the drink in his mouth momentarily, and then swallowed. The look on his face was one of bafflement. He tried another sip, and the look in his eyes was very peculiar.

'Tony," asked Maya, "are you all right?"

"Fan-*tas*-tic!" he said with satisfaction. "Who said this wasn't fit for human consumption?"

Maya couldn't resist a joke as Tony filled glasses for them all. "Who said you were human?" she said, laughing.

CHAPTER THIRTEEN

It was less than a week after the Moon Base had survived the firestorm when an aerial geological survey pinpointed a new seam of tiranium near the crater Copernicus. A large fireball collision had split open one of the old lunar rills like a ripe peach. There, deep in the basalt, was a rich vein of the dreadfully essential element. In time even that supply would run out, and they would have to continue to search for the next source in the meantime. But at last they could operate all the Alpha systems, including those just for leisure and relaxation. For the base personnel it was a welcome day when the recreation room cinema started showing films again, even though they had seen every one in the library a dozen times already.

As life relaxed, the daily routine became almost boring, and long weeks without incident slipped by. Social events began to re-assert their importance in the Alphans' personal life, and dances were scheduled to help things along.

Maya joined Helena in her room one afternoon, dressed in a shimmering rainbow-colored gown draped to the floor. Her hair was up in an elaborate baroque of curls and knots and tinted a vibrant pink.

"Tell me, Helena," Maya asked as she swept through the door, "what do you think?"

Helena took in the stunning effect. Evidently the special preparations were in honor of a dinner party that was being held in the evening. The dress was magnificent, but Helena frowned as she considered the hairstyle.

"Is something not right?" Maya asked perceptively.

"You look marvellous, but your hair ... it's just not quite correct with that gown."

Maya pouted as she considered the criticism, then she smiled and there was a twinkle in her eye. The construction of pink curls began to blur and grow pale. An opaque light swirled mistily around Maya's head, and the next thing Helena could clearly see was a shower of golden ringlets, a classical Grecian look, coming into focus.

"Like it now?" Maya asked cheerfully.

Helena nodded. 'What's more important ... Tony will like it."

With a regal wave of dismissal, Maya sniffed. "Tony? You think I care what Tony likes?"

Helena laughed at the very unconvincing pretence. The affection between the handsome Italian and the lovely Psychon grew stronger every day. She was half expecting an announcement of an engagement before long. Her thought was piercingly interrupted.

The alarm sound had a distinctively long and drawn-out whooping tone to it. Helena had not heard that particular warning sound for so long, she had to think a moment to recall what it meant.

"That's the automatic life support malfunction warning!" she explained to Maya.

"We'd better get to Command Center," she replied and stepped smartly toward the door.

Tony Verdeschi had been going over the details of replenishing the tiranium stores in the Eagle propulsion units when the alarm started to sound. He too, had to think a moment to remember the coded signal, but Yasko was running a check on it almost instantly. She expected to see an immediate indication of something like an oxygen leak or a thermostat failure. Instead, all the data showed normal ecological conditions in all areas.

"What is it?" Tony shouted over to her.

"I can't find anything wrong yet," she replied. "I'll run a test on the alarm system." It only took seconds before she had an answer. "It looks like the alarm circuit has gone haywire. It must have set itself off."

"Can you pinpoint the fault?"

Suddenly the room was flooded by the sound of another siren . . . a rising and falling howl that made Alan Carter's ears ache. As a pilot he knew that sound very well . . . it meant a fire in the fuel stores.

Yasko was quick to check on it. "Now it's a section F malfunction," she said, noting that all other instruments said things were perfectly normal at the fuel depot.

Several other alarm systems went off, horns, bells, and whistles jarring against each other in a pandemonium of noise. Lights were blipping madly all over the consoles, trying to call attention to seemingly nonexistent disasters. Koenig came charging into the room just ahead of Helena and Maya.

"What the devil's going on?" he shouted to Verdeschi, barely making himself heard.

Tony had double-checked Yasko's data on the printout. "Malfunction main electronics!" He looked up. "Whatever the problem is, it seems to be spreading."

"Cut off those alarms!"

An incredible silence descended on the Command Center as Tony pressed the override button. The torrent of decibels had numbed everyone's hearing so badly that Koenig still had to speak loudly to be heard.

"Give me a visual check of sections . . . up on the big screen, in order of priority rating. I want to see for certain that there's nothing wrong. Heaven only knows there's likely to be after all that confusion."

They looked up to the screen in anticipation but saw only a zigzagging pattern of vivid colors. Yasko tried to get a picture on the optional channels.

"Malfunction spreading to video systems," Tony reported.

Koenig felt an alarm all his own go off then, a warning tingle of danger in the back of his brain. "Reset," he ordered.

Yasko tried putting the Command Center power through on an alternative circuit, but to no avail. "Negative."

Even as she spoke, the scramble of light on the screen began to dip and fade. All around the room the myriad bulbs of brightness on console boards began to go out.

"Power fading fast!" Tony reported. "Switching to emergency power." He tried to change over, but there was no response. Horrified, he looked at Koenig for further instructions.

"Yasko," Koenig asked, steeling his expression, "status report?"

Very calmly and regretfully she told him the worst. "Complete power failure. Malfunction Systems A through G. Malfunction complete life support."

As his mind raced, wondering what his next decision would have to be, Koenig noticed that a strange aura of light had pervaded the room. At first it seemed to be coming from the walls, part of the fading glow of Alpha's control boards' working illumination. Then, as he swivelled his head, he saw that there was an actual point of brilliance emerging from a point in midair in the room's center.

While he watched it, he realized with dread that he was petrified. Quite literally, he was frozen into one position and could not move a muscle. Within the field of his vision he could see that Tony and Maya were in the same condition and could presume everyone else in the center was, too.

The light blazed and then cohered into the shape of a lovely young girl with a fresh-complexioned, smiling face framed with short, dark hair. She was dressed only in a light, semi-transparent shift that revealed an athletic and perfectly formed body.

She seemed to beam with triumph as she looked around the room and inspected the helpless Alphans. Only then did she turn to the Commander and, by no more gesture than a nod, release him from his bondage. Koenig had to steady himself quickly on the edge of a chair until his equilibrium came back, but his first anxious thoughts were for the rest of the Alphans frozen in their stances.

"They will be all right," the girl reassured him in a perfectly—an almost too perfectly—inflected voice. He was more startled by the fact that she seemed to read his thoughts.

At the same time, the other Alphans stirred from immobility and blinked in confusion at the attractive stranger that had come from nowhere.

"Who are you?" Koenig asked.

"I am Zamara . . . of the planet Vega." She looked around the quizzical faces with a kind of arrogance. "Your small world has entered our sphere of influence. You are . . .?"

"Commander John Koenig. We are in your . . . 'sphere of influence' by accident, and with no hostile intent."

Zamara nodded imperiously. "I accept your explanation."

"However," Koenig said in a harsher voice, feeling resentful of the visitor's attitude, "if you don't unlock our systems immediately I will be forced to—"

The stranger whirled around with a flashing stare. "Your systems are being held in an electro force field. It can also be used, as you have experienced, to affect your individual nerve centers."

"That can be dangerous," Helena warned. "Our nervous systems are delicately balanced."

Zamara dismissed the concern. "There will be no lasting effects, I assure you. And for the present I will allow your habitat minimum life support power." She looked back at Koenig. "I will adjust the control so that you can survive for forty-eight hours."

Koenig leaned forward menacingly, anger reddening his face. "That seems like a very dangerous game to play. What exactly is the purpose of it?"

The smile on Zamara's face was very diplomatic, but coldly artificial. "We mean you no harm . . . we only want to assure your cooperation. It will be necessary for two of you to return with me to Vega. During the period of their visit we do not want any interference with our plans."

"The best way to assure our cooperation is to give us back the control of our systems and to explain fully what you want."

Tactfully avoiding the Commander's hard stare, Zamara shook her head. "This is the only way to guarantee your help. But don't worry, whoever comes with me will be returned after assisting us. I give you the assurance of the people of Vega—and besides, you have no choice."

Thinking quickly, Koenig came to the conclusion that, like it or not, they were momentarily at the mercy of this strange woman. Without knowing what kind of help they were expected to provide, cooperation would be the expedient course to take. If there were only forty-eight hours of life left for Alpha, it would be best to get started immediately. His mind made up, he stepped toward . Zamara.

"All right," he said, "let's go."

Zamara shook her head. "I do not think you are suitable." She looked slowly around the rest of the personnel and pointed at Helena and then at Verdeschi. "I choose you . . . and you."

"Now just a minute!" Koenig stormed. "I'm not letting—" He stopped in mid-sentence, a finger of emphasis half-raised. Zamara had immobilized him again.

Turning back to Tony and Helena, Zamara snapped her fingers to get their concerned attention off the statue-like Koenig. "We will travel by positronic transfer," she announced. "Just relax and let your mind go blank. You'll be there before you know it."

Tony shrugged and closed his eyes, working to clear his thoughts. Helena felt unsure, dreading leaving Alpha behind for the unknown. Besides, even though she had seen the materialization of Zamara, she felt terribly foolish standing in the middle of the Command Center waiting to disappear in a puff of smoke.

"If you value the lives of your friends," Zamara said to her harshly, bringing the problem down to grim reality, "you will do it."

Helena accordingly closed her eyes, joining Tony in the attempt to empty her head of thoughts. It didn't feel as though she was succeeding, and she knew, with exasperation, that she would be not a little embarrassed when she opened her eyes and asked why it wasn't working.

Koenig, meanwhile, was feeling dreadful. There he was, uselessly rigid, and in front of his very eyes, Tony and Helena had just vanished from sight. Zamara waited till they were gone and then nodded to release him again.

"I want a channel of communication opened," he snapped, "so that we can stay in contact."

Zamara considered the request for a moment and then broke into her humorless smile. Walking over to the Command control board she nodded and the transmitter light flicked on.

"Your radio is now functioning," she announced and then evaporated without a sound.

The first thing Helena became aware of was the sound of a flock of cooing doves. Next came the scent of flowers . . . an exotic abundance of them. She opened her eyes in disbelief and beheld a lush and sylvan garden. All around her bloomed beautifully colorful plants and trees bowed down under a plentiful crop of strange fruits. Standing just next to her and equally confused was Tony.

Gradually they recovered from their wonder and began to move around the garden. High above them there was a ceiling so it appeared they were in a controlled environment. Tony spotted an oval window and walked across to see what the outside conditions were like, but the glass seemed caked in frost on the exterior and he couldn't make out any details.

Helena strolled near the edge of the clearing and looked back into the shrubbery to see if there was a path leading through it. She reached her hand out and pushed aside a large flat leaf—and cried out in fear.

Staring out at her was a face. It was stark white, the eyes nothing more than dark round holes and the skin unlined and thick, like the bloated flesh of a drowned man. A rough gray garment covered the rest of the body with the numeral 8 inscribed on it in red.

A strong and very cultivated voice spoke from just behind her. "Did it startle you?"

Spinning around, Helena saw a tall and handsome man leaning against the trunk of a nearby tree. Like Zamara's, his dress was brief and semi-transparent, scarcely hiding his lithe and well-proportioned physique. Without taking his eyes off Helena, he spoke to the thing behind the shrubbery.

"Bring food for our guests." He smiled and walked closer. "I am Zarl. I hope your stay on Vega is very . . . pleasurable."

Tony was just about to step away from the window and join them when a haze of light appeared in front of him. In a moment it had materialized into Zamara. With the ease of someone very used to such a dramatic form of travelling, she spoke to him as if she had been there all the time.

"Outside, the temperature is always sub-zero and the atmosphere too thin for human comfort. I am sure you will find all you desire inside our enclosed city."

It completely surprised Tony that her ambiguous words of welcome should be delivered with such an openly suggestive look. He had expected to encounter unusual social codes on an alien planet, but he distrusted the calculated temptation that the pretty girl was exuding. In spite of his caution, however, his Latin blood was feeling just the least bit tempted.

At the edge of the clearing three of the odd humanoids with white faces appeared carrying trays of food and drink. Each of them had a different number printed in red on his gray uniform. Close behind them came several other Vegans, each of them as attractive and pleasingly shaped as Zarl and Zamara.

Tony and Helena took the seats indicated at either side of a long low table. The Vegas joined them, settling gracefully on plump, delicately brocaded cushions.

"Refresh yourselves," invited Zarl.

The gruesomely ugly things moved around the table and began to serve food. As one bent down uncomfortably close to Helena, she heard an anxious whisper in her ear.

"Whatever happens, do not react as they expect."

Helena kept her face impassive and said, "Thank you," as if for the service.

"There is no need to thank a number," explained Zarl.

"Are they robots or something?" asked Tony.

"Hmm, not really. Automatons is more precise."

The same one, the thing with the number 8 on its chest, returned to Helena's side and poured a sparkling red wine into her goblet. This time it whispered, "If you show aggression, they will kill you."

It moved quickly away, and Helena hid her surprise by lifting a delicious-looking red vegetable to her mouth. She bit into the soft skin and was astonished to discover that it had a flavor like old window putty.

133

"Is the food to your liking?" asked Zarl.

Helena made herself nod. "Yes, it's very unusual."

"You are a liar!" Zamara hissed at her. "It sticks in your throat, you decrepit hag."

Tony was stunned by the outburst and even more surprised that Helena seemed totally unaffected by it. Zarl pushed one of the dishes toward him, and he decided the best way to smooth over the moment was to try something himself. As he raised the morsel up to his tongue, Helena spoke to him anxiously.

"The food *is* absolutely delicious, Tony."

He detected an element of caution in her voice. It became clearer as he chewed the food and found out it had a flavor like unwashed socks. He smiled with great effort.

"Delicious."

This time it was Zarl who reacted. "You foul-mouthed, lying cretin!"

Tony felt the hackles on his neck rise and an irrepressible surge of anger.

"You are our guest," Zarl continued, his tone provocatively changing from the friendly to the insulting, "so feel free to do as you like. Eat the food! Throw it in my face! Whatever you want." Zarl leaned forward with a sneer. "But at least try to act like a man . . . not a cringing, spineless—"

Without even thinking about it, Tony had closed his fingers around the edge of the heavy plate in front of him. He started to lift it up, ready to smash it into Zarl's leering face.

Quickly Helena leaned over the table and took the plate from Tony's hand. "We are not used to such hot food," she said charmingly to the Vegans, and then meaningfully to Tony, "Cool it!"

He settled back down, getting the message, but wondering what was going on.

Koenig waited impatiently as Yasko tried to raise an answer from Vega on the radio. The only response was a depressing silence.

134

"She lied to us," he said to Maya. "They're not letting us communicate."

Maya sighed, frowning with worry about Tony and Helena. "If she lied to us about that, then she lied about . . ."

The Commander's thoughts were there ahead of her. "We've got to get down to Vega!"

Koenig thought to himself that it was all very well to make strong statements, but just how he'd back that one up, he wasn't sure. They weren't likely to go anywhere without power. He had ordered a thorough search of the Moon Base just on the chance that some simple device had been planted which was actually neutralizing all the electronics. So far, there had been nothing discovered except that conditions were getting worse.

"What's the life support situation?" he asked Maya nervously.

"Critical losses of heat and oxygen. I would say we now have forty-two hours left—maximum."

Koenig thumped the desk in frustration. Perhaps it now all depended on Alan Carter and the men he took with him to try to reach the Eagles. If they could bring back one of the power packs, the base might still have a chance. Of course, it was possible that the Eagles had been "fixed," as well. In that case they were totally at the mercy of the Vegan's promises . . . promises that were proving very unreliable so far.

Helena and Tony stood reflectively inside their guest room in the Vegan city. They had been escorted there by Zari and told to make themselves comfortable. Tony had been increasingly mystified as Helena said how pleasant and comfortable the accommodation looked, and Zarl had simply looked frustrated.

After the door had slid shut behind them, the lock clicking loudly, Tony blew out a breath of exasperation. The room was hardly larger than a closet and had solid walls of cold, gray stone. The only opening was the sealed door and the only furniture a flat, hard slab.

Helena took her comlock in her hand and tried to

call the Moon Base. "Doctor Russell calling Alpha. Come in, Alpha."

"Forget it, Helena," Tony said and took out his stun-gun, which he thought was more likely to help them solve the situation.

"No, Tony," Helena warned him. "That's what they want. One of the numbers warned me."

"If we start believing robots—"

"I believe this one," she said firmly. "It said if we show aggression, they will kill us. You have to admit they seem to be setting out to provoke us as much as possible."

"But why?"

"There's only one way to get some answers." She nodded at the door. "We've got to find that number."

Tony considered and agreed that it seemed the best course available to them. He clicked his gun onto the laser beam and aimed at the bolts on the inside of the cell door that marked the location of the lock. Two good blasts of the beam, and the door swung easily open.

The corridors of the Vegan city were scantily occupied so that Helena and Tony had little difficulty moving along them unobserved. The population of the planet seemed very low, but since they were confined to the limits of the cave-hewn city, Helena reckoned that they must have carefully controlled the population growth.

After dodging out of sight when several Vegans passed by, they finally saw a number walking along on its own. Carefully they followed it and before long saw it push open a door and go through. They paused, then followed, finding themselves in a much less improved cave area on a downward-leading slope.

They shuffled down the sandy incline, trying to avoid the cold water dripping from stalactites overhead. The number walked slowly ahead of them, easy to keep up with and apparently not aware that they were behind it.

In a few minutes they had dropped down about a hundred feet below the level of the city. The air was cold, moist, and uncomfortable, and the light a weak yellow gloom. They stepped around one more corner in the cave tunnel and saw before them a large, open cavern.

Looking up at them with their frighteningly blank white faces was a group of a dozen numbers. They were sitting with weary postures on low rocks that bordered a bubbling pool of a natural hot spring.

Helena stepped bravely forward, Tony right beside her with his gun ready for trouble.

"We come as friends," said Helena.

The numbers stared silently.

"I want to speak to the one who warned me," Helena tried again. "We need your help . . . maybe we can help each other."

The numbers still did not speak or move. Almost a minute passed of tense expectation, and then one of them stood up slowly. He raised a hand to his face and pinched the skin hard between his fingers. With a sucking sound and a snap he pulled the white covering away and revealed a perfectly ordinary, if very sad, middle-aged man's face.

"You're . . . you're not androids?" asked Tony.

"No," the man answered, "they're the androids. We're the humans."

CHAPTER FOURTEEN

Sitting near the steaming pool, Helena could understand why the numbers—the people—chose to gather in this cavern. The heat of the spring water provided at least a little comfort.

The number who had revealed his face, the one with the red 8 on his chest, explained fully the situation on Vega. Tony and Helena both listened raptly to his troubled tale.

"It was many years ago that we built the first androids, linking them to an extremely advanced and powerful computer. We thought to free ourselves completely from the drudgery of routine labor so that our civilization could advance in the fields of art and culture. We were prevented from doing so throughout our history by struggling to survive on the planet's surface." The man shook his balding head. "But the computer was smarter than we expected. It programmed the androids with more complex ideas than we intended and used them to build improvements on itself so that it came to control all of our city."

"A self-generating system?" asked Tony.

"Yes. The cycle continued until the crude robots we started with became the perfect humanoid form you see today. They are all psychically linked to the master computer and to each other—separate parts of one great mind—a diabolical one."

"But they express emotions . . . as individuals?" Helena asked, recalling the look of interest Zarl had given her when she first arrived.

"They imitate the attitude without knowing the feeling. The only emotions they cannot portray are love and hate. Those they have not yet learned."

Helena thought for a moment, remembering again the look on Zarl's face. There had been something more to it than just a portrayal, but what? And how?

"Why do you cover your faces?" asked Tony, looking around at the other unpleasant masks.

"So that if we are caught off-guard we will not reveal strong emotions."

Feeling increasingly confused, Helena said, "But if they want to see you, surely all they have to do is rip the masks off your faces?"

138

"No, they cannot now employ violence or force. We have never displayed it in their presence, so they have no experience by which to create an imitation."

Eight's eyes took on a fatalistic sorrow. "They would like very much to kill us, but they can't. They don't possess the emotional pattern of anger or aggression. That is what they want to learn from you . . . how to kill."

Helena shook her head. "But why do they want to kill you? What is the point?"

"As long as we live, we are a threat to them. They know and fear human ingenuity. While we live, there is a chance we might find some way of reaching the master computer and putting an end to them."

"Where is this . . ." Tony leaned forward anxiously, sensing an opportunity, "this master computer? Is it well guarded?"

Number 8 pointed across the cave, to the opposite end from where they had entered. "There is a tunnel back there that goes straight up to it. But there is no point. It's protected by an impenetrable force screen. So they have no need for guards."

Tony got to his feet and helped Helena. "Thanks," he said, "I think we'll go and have a crack at it. Sounds like our only hope at the moment."

"Remember," Number 8 shouted after them. "Do not show them violence, whatever they do. Otherwise they will kill us all!"

The master computer of Vega pulsed and bubbled inside its glistening array of bending, looping tubes. Like a giant altar to self-important intellect, it sat in the middle of an expansive domed room, a large space of polished tiles on every side. Helena and Tony looked up at it with a mixture of scientific appreciation and human fear as they approached. A computer based on liquid chemical circuitry was obviously a staggering accomplishment.

Abruptly Tony rocked back on his heels, feeling as though he had been run into by an invisible and very heavy sandbag. He shook his head to clear it as Helena reached out to steady him.

"I'm all right," he said. "It's a strong force field ... but at least it's not as vicious as some I've experienced."

He took out his gun and turned the laser ray up to full power. The beam of pure light hummed out and struck the force field in a blaze of sparks. It didn't appear to have any other effect.

"You're wasting your time."

Helena and Tony both jumped with surprise when the voice of Zarl sounded close behind them. They turned around to face both him and a smirking Zamara.

Zarl added, "Not all the power of your Moon Base could scratch that shield."

"You were not supposed to leave your quarters," Zamara stated, stepping forward. "Why have you come here to the computer? What did you hope to achieve?"

Tony felt a wave of resentment rush through him ... that she should dare to question the urge for gaining freedom that any person held prisoner would feel. Then he looked at Helena, and the message in her eyes was a timely reminder to keep calm.

"We were worried about our friends. We were trying to find a way to get to them," he said with forced politeness.

Helena was keeping a close watch on Zarl, catching his occasional sidelong looks. She was still certain that there was the seed of a real emotion down there ... if only she could find the way to encourage it.

She stepped closer to him and asked softly, "Please ... release us ... and the Moon Base."

The mask of arrogance drained away from Zarl's face, and a look of doubt took its place. "Perhaps ..."—he looked at Zamara—"perhaps there's another way?"

"No!" she said harshly, and Zarl obediently resumed his own severe attitude.

"If you're so worried about your friends, why don't you go back and see them?" His voice was cutting once again.

"Go back? But how?"

Zamara laughed, short and sharp. "They never learn, do they? To go back all you have to do is clear your mind and the positronic transfer will take you where you are inclined to go."

Helena and Tony exchanged glances of doubt, wondering whether the Vegan androids were setting them up for some further mockery. They both knew that there was enough of a chance that they weren't able to miss the opportunity. They shut their eyes and strained to blank out their thoughts.

As Helena's wide-opened gaze adjusted itself, she saw around her the unmistakeably bright and functioning lights of Alpha Command Center. Just behind her, Tony was letting his own senses adjust, and except for him, there was no one else in the room.

Tony was feeling momentarily disconnected by the effect of the positronic travel technique, but as soon as he recognized where he was, he gushed with delight. Then he recognized that all the circuits looked back to normal and felt even better. With full facilities restored and with a chance of working out a plan with the rest of the Moon Base senior officers, he felt sure they could thwart the Vegan scheme.

Helena's worried question abruptly halted the flow of his confidence. "Where is everybody, Tony?"

Leaping to the control panel, Tony punched communications buttons. "Weapons Section . . . Weapons Section." He pressed some more. "Petrov? Are you at your station, Petrov?" He looked around in confusion at Helena while continuing to try. "Medical Section? Doctor Vincent, are you there?"

Unable to stand idly by any longer, Helena ran out of the room and down the corridor. She quickly reached the door with the sign on it, "Commander's Quarters." With a musical chime of her comlock the door slid open for her.

"John!" she shouted. "John!"

Only a terrible silence answered her. In ever rising

141

fear she ran out again and looked into several other nearby rooms before returning to the Command Center. She didn't need to tell Tony what she had found.

"They must have been sent down somehow . . . they must be on Vega," he said with a shake of his head. He had been wondering at the twisted cruelty of the Vegans to let them know they could come back to Alpha just as they were somehow enticing all the other Alphans to Vega.

"We've got to get back," Helena said quickly.

"How?"

"The same way as before. Blank our minds and let the positronic process take us back."

Neither of them hesitated this time, closing their eyelids and waiting expectantly for the old tingle of displacement that would tell them they had arrived. But this time, there was nothing. They opened their eyes to the same old acrylic walls of Moon Base.

"They must have somehow turned off the power for the positronic system. We can't go back!" Tony turned to the computer console and got it to feed a diagram of the local star system up to the big screen. They located the position of the Moon by a flashing light and then checked on the location of Vega. There seemed to be a gap between the two of over a light-year, and it was constantly increasing.

Helena was shattered. "A light-year? Then we'll never see the others again!"

"We'll never see anybody again," Tony said unhappily, "except each other."

Helena moved listlessly around the space in her own room. Arrayed on a worktop surface was a collection of various medications which she had been inventorying at the moment when she had been interrupted by Maya's visit . . . only hours before, though it seemed like days.

She picked up one of the bottles that contained a mild tranquilizer and took one of the small green pills out. Popping it into her mouth, she washed it down with a swallow of water from a small cup. Anticipating that the edge would soon be taken off her nerves, she went over to her voice recorder. She felt obliged to make some kind of log entry of what had happened to them.

"Moon Base Alpha..." she said somberly. "Status report... Doctor Russell recording. We do not know what has happened to John Koenig, Alan Carter... in fact, all of the Moon Base personnel. Tony Verdeschi and I are alone in Alpha. All systems are now functioning, but we have not been able to establish contact with Vega, where we suspect the other Alphans have been taken. The anticipation of future loneliness is having a terrible effect on both Tony and me... as well as the thought of losing... of never..." Helena felt herself hesitate as the very personal sense of loss that she and Tony felt proved too difficult to commit to record in such a coolly routine way.

She turned off the recorder and walked back to her desk. There amidst the pill bottles was a plastic cup of steaming coffee. Tony had brought it in for her about five minutes before and had let her know how unsuccessfully his attempts to make radio contact with Vega were going. Nor could he solve the mystery of their sudden and enormous acceleration away from the planet.

Helena picked up the cup and turned to walk back and have another try at recording her report. A flash of brightness caught her eye... a small twist of red paper in the bottom of the white disposal bin on the floor. That morning, she knew, the bin had been empty and she knew her own pharmacopeia well enough to recognize the paper as the wrapper off a dexetrol tablet, a very potent sedative. She recalled that Tony had stood by the desk for a few minutes, talking, after he had brought the coffee.

Sniffing at the cup of coffee, penetrating the smell of the drink itself, Helena could clearly detect something chemically bitter. With growing alarm she walked across the room to the small adjoining washroom and emptied the cup down the drain.

She did not notice the small strip of perspex that was part of the moulded contour of the wall... as it slid open and revealed a very cleverly concealed viewing gap. In the darkness behind it a well-satisfied pair of eyes seemed to gleam with anticipated triumph.

....

Tony could think of nothing else to try but to keep up a barrage of broadcasts back toward the disappearing dot of Vega. The computer could give him no reason at all for the sudden jump in either space or time that they had undergone. He could only presume that some effect of the positronic method of travel had placed them on Alpha months in the future and their fate was now sealed.

His voice had grown tired, calling out fruitlessly into space. He pressed a button that would automatically broadcast a distress code on all frequencies. If they were going to be heard at all, that would be the only way. He considered one morbid possibility . . . that the Vegans had achieved their aim of getting the Alphans to show them violence. After all, there were enough hotheads in the crew for them to find one that couldn't resist being provoked . . . certainly not without prior warning of the scheme. By now the androids could have had their lesson in violence and used it to kill all the humans, native and Alphan, that were on Vega. And no doubt, Maya, too, his beloved Psychon.

His unhappy daydream was interrupted suddenly, in a crudely ironic fashion—by the thing that had started the grim tragedy in the first place. The life support malfunction alarm went off. Tony punched a quick series of codes into the computer and this time could clearly see that it wasn't a faulty circuit—the oxygen in the Moon Base really was disappearing . . . from all areas and *very* quickly.

He called through to Helena's room. "Helena? Helena, are you there?" When there was no reply, he tried the Medical Section. "Helena! Answer me, Helena! We are losing our atmosphere . . ."

Even as he spoke, he could feel himself starting to gasp, the first uncomfortable onset of oxygen deprivation. The computer was reporting on the source of the fault and located it in the life support operations room.

He knew there was no more time to try to find Helena.
He had to go and see if he could repair the fault. At the
rate air was being lost, they had only minutes before they
would both die from suffocation, no matter what part of
the Moon Base they were in.

CHAPTER FIFTEEN

It was difficult moving down the corridor at all, let
alone in a hurry. Tony felt as though his legs had turned
to soft rubber, and the walls seemed to be suspended on
ropes so that they swung crazily from side to side. He
drove himself on, knowing he hadn't a second to spare.

The door of the life support center was ahead of him,
only a dozen paces away. He moved toward it with such
concentration that he didn't notice when the door of the
hydrophonics section that he had just passed eased open.
Nor did he see Helena stagger out and walk in the other
direction, holding herself up against the wall as she went
to the Command Center. Clutched nervously in her hand
was a stun-gun.

As soon as he was inside the door, his eyes immediately saw the door of the master control panel standing
open. He knew that not many Alpha staff members had
the necessary authority in their comlock key frequency
to unlock it. But of course, both he and Helena were
among the few.

Inside the panel he found that the handle to empty
the entire base of its artificial atmosphere had been
pulled. With fading strength he pushed it back into place

145

and heard immediately the low hissing of air replacement as the alarm sound ceased.

Recovering his strength, he relocked the panel and turned to start back to the Command Center. On second thought, and very reluctantly, he took out his stun-gun and held it at the ready before he left the room.

Helena had checked as quickly as she could to see exactly what Tony had been up to while she was supposed to have been drugged in deep sleep. As far as she could tell, he had been doing his best to make radio contact with Vega, but there was no indication of a reply. Evidently he had something else in mind, too, something that had caused a fault in the base's oxygen supply. Maybe he had intended just to siphon the air from her bedroom and finish her off, and it had gone wrong. There was no way to tell, but she had to suspect the worst.

As the door behind Helena slid open, she spun around, raising her gun. She froze in icy fear as she saw Tony crouched just over the threshold, aiming at her with his own weapon.

After a heart-stopping moment, she said in a tensely terrified voice, "Tony . . . I don't want to shoot you. Put down your gun."

He didn't answer but moved slowly toward her, keeping his gun steady.

"Tony," she pleaded, "drop it, please."

By her fright and the tears of regret in her eyes, Tony could tell that whatever was wrong with Helena, she wasn't irredeemable. "Easy, Helena," he said soothingly, "I only want to help you."

Trying to humor him, trying to calm him any way she could, Helena replied, "Yes, I know that, Tony. That's why you put the dexotrol in my coffee. You wanted to calm me down . . . but if you want to do that, then just put your gun away."

Verdeschi wasn't sure what she was talking about, but expected it must be part of whatever delusion she was under that had made her let out the base's oxygen. "Is that why you sabotaged the life support system?" he asked.

"Me?" she replied with incredulity. "Tony, listen to me. You're hallucinating. I didn't sabotage the life support system. I've not been near it. Why would I do that? I'd be killing myself."

Tony paused thoughtfully. "I don't know why you did it. The situation we're in now must be causing you a lot of stress. People do strange things when they're despondent . . . lonely . . ."

"No, Tony." Helena said adamantly. "No."

"There's only the two of us on Alpha . . . and I've been in the Command Center all the time. It had to be you."

"But it had to be *you* that put a drug in my coffee!"

Tony's eyes suddenly lit up with a flash of inspiration. An outrageous suspicion came into bloom and began to grow from possibility to probability in the space of a few seconds. Helena saw the idea cross his face and caught it instantly.

"That is, it had to be you unless there are more than two of us on Alpha." She no more had to speak the thought than to be convinced of it. With a big smile at Tony she put her gun away and laughed. "Can you imagine that those silly Vegans thought they could make us hate each other?"

Tony's guffaw echoed around the room, his elation feeling very genuine. Even though they were still in the Vegans' clutches, at least he knew Helena was not going mad . . . and also that there was still a chance that they could get back to the real Moon Base Alpha.

"How about that?" he said. "They don't know how much fun we have playing their little games."

Helena shouted out cheerily. "Zarl! Zamara! You can show yourselves. The game's over."

A section of the wall just below the big screen slid open, and from behind the false panelling stepped the two androids, looking piqued with the failure of their elaborate ruse.

"So you think it's a game, do you?" asked Zamara.

147

"Isn't it?" laughed Tony. "You built all this . . . a full replica of Alpha . . . down to every detail. You gambled that, and lost."

Zamara turned on her heels and stalked away. "This time!" she shouted, and in a blur of light, she disappeared before she got to the exit.

Koenig was checking the latest condition reports in the Command Center when the security guard came rushing in to get him. The air in the room, as throughout the base, was chilly and rapidly getting very stale. Over half the time they had left to live had passed . . . and they were no nearer a solution.

Carter had failed to get through to the Eagles. There was no way to operate the travel tubes, and even the electrics that controlled the spacesuit functions were on the blink. All ionic transfer on Luna was being blocked by the force field so that electric current just couldn't flow. Most likely the Eagles would be powerless as well.

Alan got the urgent message from the security man and shouted it across to Koenig. "Commander! There's an alien in the recreation area!"

Koenig was on his feet and running, with Carter and Maya close behind. From the open doors of the rec room he could hear the loud strains of Beethoven's *Ninth Symphony*. He dashed inside just as they stopped, in mid-chord.

Zamara was standing by the cassette library and had just taken the music tape off the machine. She turned and looked at him expressionlessly as he walked closer.

"Where are they?" he asked.

"They are safe," she said. Moving farther along, she came to the shelves of the microfilm library . . . thousands and thousands of the world's greatest books stored on tiny spools of celluloid. She chose one and slid it into the viewing machine.

"Why have you come back?" asked Koenig.

Zamara set the viewer into action, and turned on to fast forward play, usually used to hurry to the later pages in a reference book. Koenig thought for a moment that the Vegan simply didn't understand the controls of the machine, but then he gathered with surprise that she was apparently reading them as they flipped past in a blur.

"We needed . . . additional material," she explained, without looking away.

Out of the corner of his eye Koenig saw Carter start to sneak out his stun-gun and motioned for him to put it away. Without knowing what was happening to Helena and Tony they couldn't risk taking forceful action.

Zamara changed the microtape in the viewer for another one, unaware of how close she had come to getting all the information that she needed. As the new film whizzed through, she nodded appreciatively. "Ahh . . . Julius Caesar by William Shakespeare . . . and here is a story of murder." She took the microfilm out. "Et tu, Brute."

"You have an eidetic memory," commented Koenig.

"I have reviewed the pages. They killed Caesar. Why?"

Puzzled by her interest, Koenig shrugged. "It was a political act."

"Are you on Alpha of a political nature?"

Koenig was feeling increasingly impatient. "No."

Looking for another film, Zamara said quietly, "Then we do not want Julius Caesar."

"What do you want?"

Zamara ignored the question and selected another book. The pages played through the viewer with great speed, and Zamara caught her breath with interest. "Now, that is interesting," she said.

Koenig moved closer. "What is it?"

"Othello," she said, and looked him over with curiosity. "So jealousy, too, makes humans kill?"

"Yes, Zamara, it can." Koenig wanted to dispose of this inexplicable exploration of the darker side of human nature. There was quite enough of a real life-or-death struggle going on without delving into fiction. "It depends on how strongly two people care about each other. Now, how long will it be before Helena and Tony—"

"That is all we need to know," Zamara cut him short.

149

Exasperated, he asked, "What do you need to know?"

"That jealousy will create violence . . . that lovers can be made jealous enough to hurt and kill."

As Zamara began to dematerialize, Koenig finally began to put together the clues of the conversation. He couldn't find a definite conclusion, but he was close enough to understand what was on the Vegan's mind. That alone was enough to frighten him badly.

"Zamara!" he yelled. "It won't work . . . not with Helena and Tony!"

The Vegan reappeared instantly, pouting with annoyance. "But why not?" she demanded.

"It only applies to lovers, and Tony and Helena are not in love with each other."

The Vegan considered this information carefully, like a scientist weighing an additional fact for a new theory of physics. She looked at Koenig with sudden keen perception. "Then whom do they love?"

Koenig didn't know what he was letting himself in for, but even if it hadn't been the truth, he would have answered as he did . . . for the sake of getting in a position to deal with the situation in person. "I love Helena," he said, as the Vegan expected. "And Tony loves Maya." The Psychon lowered her head with embarrassment, but Koenig knew this was no time for oversensitivity. Maya's talents could well be useful to them down on Vega, if that was where they were about to be invited to.

There was quite a crowd waiting in the tropical garden when Zamara returned with Koenig and Maya. The greeting between John and Helena and between Tony and Maya reaffirmed Zamara's belief that this time her plan would work.

Stepping in front of Zarl and the others, she asked, "You have read the play *Othello*?"

Koenig looked up at this, knowing full well that he had just seen Zamara read the drama on Alpha . . . why ask them? As the Vegans all nodded in unison and Helena whispered the single word "androids" into his ear, he began to understand.

150

Zarl said, "Through you . . . we all did."

"This time we know the way," Zamara announced, and the Vegans moved swiftly away into the edges of the clearing and began to bring out large, soft cushions, flagons of wine, and musical instruments.

Holding him tighter with growing worry about what the Vegans would try next, Helena whispered to Koenig, "John, they're planning to use you."

"Yes, as Othello," Koenig agreed, "only the devil knows why, or how."

Tony had moved cautiously over to the Commander's side and spoke low enough for only him to hear. "Because they have no experience of violence or killing of their own. They want to make you show them how . . . then they'll kill us all." Koenig shot him a look of appalled surprise. Keeping his voice low, Tony added, "The only hope we have of beating them is to get to the main computer. It's through the tunnel on the other side of the grove, but it's protected by a force shield. If we could get to it we could finish them all because they're telepathically linked."

Maya had heard the latter part of Tony's explanation and with a nod of her head to indicate her intentions moved toward a flock of dove-like birds rustling in the bushes. Koenig signalled that he knew what she was up to and turned to inspect the Vegans' preparations. The cushions were arranged, incense sticks were burning, and the lights had been turned down to soft, sensuous mellowness. Good cover for Maya's change, Koenig knew.

As a slow and persistent drumbeat began, Zamara walked over to the Alphans. She was too full of the certainty of success to notice that Maya was missing.

As Zarl joined her, she explained, "Soon you will make love to the woman Helena. Her lover will become enraged, and we will have won."

"Through consuming jealousy . . ."

"Yes." Zamara's eyes gleamed with coming victory. "It was all there. Othello and Desdemona . . . the scheming Iago twisting a man's love into violent jealousy . . . enough to kill."

151

Koenig and Helena looked at each other and with their eyes confirmed their feelings for each other. The emotion that was about to become the fuel for a painful and deadly test of willpower was for the moment their only comfort.

CHAPTER SIXTEEN

The sound of the drum pulsed, and soft flute-like melodies rose around it like thin veils covering an erotically undulating body. The setting now in the garden was deeply and poignantly romantic, every sight, sound, and fragrance specially intended to induce desire. Helena recalled what they had been told about the androids . . . that they hadn't experienced either hate *or* love. Certainly they seemed to have come to an understanding of lust and in their physical perfection must have devoted some time to its study and practice.

Zarl looked thoughtfully at Helena and Koenig standing together. He was feeling a surge of information input that bolstered that slight aberration that set him apart from the other androids. He whispered nervously to Zamara.

"Did you see the way he looked at her?" He ignored the reprimand in Zamara's glance. "To feel something as strongly that . . . to cause this thing called jealousy . . . could we be missing something important?"

"I have told you, Zarl. The human emotion of love is a weakness . . . only hate is strength. That is why we have to learn it. Now, do what you must!"

Zarl snapped back into his proper attitude, his muscles tensing. Provocatively he walked toward Helena, his eyes devouring her with unmistakable intention. He took her hand and led her away, into the center of the grotto.

Tony whispered a warning to Koenig. "He's going to try to get to you. You'll have to be strong until Maya can get at the computer."

Koenig nodded, but already he felt his fists tightening.

"Make love to her," Zamara ordered Zarl. "Kiss her."

Helena noted the momentary hesitation as once again Zarl wrestled with his doubt. Then the strength of the androids' linked minds took over and he pulled her to him, wrapping her in his arms and pressing his lips against her neck.

A feeling of raw anger blasted through Koenig and set him trembling as he watched Helena being handled. Helena turned her face away from Zarl's insistent kisses and tried to show him how unaffected she was.

Koenig spoke out of the corner of his mouth to Tony. "How long does she think I can take this?"

Out of the shadows, Zamara suddenly came up to his other side and in a voice like a viper's hiss egged him on. "Look, Lord Othello. Observe that your Desdemona offers no resistance to save her virtue. Perhaps she finds Zarl's attention more pleasing than she wants you to know."

Koenig felt his gut muscles tense, already imagining himself running forward and pulling them apart. The music had become even more throbbing and persistent, hypnotizing both Zarl and Helena so that their movements became increasingly provocative.

Tony hovered by Koenig's side, wanting to reach out and clasp his shoulder with an indication of sympathy. He knew the gesture would also enable him to actually restrain Koenig if the pressure became too much. However, if that became necessary, then his own action of force would be enough to start the Vegans on their road to violence.

"The dance is reaching its climax," said Zamara with delight. "The time of reckoning is near."

All around the grove, the anxious eyes of the Vegans were on the couple as Zarl forced Helena to dance and turn faster. He pushed her away and pulled her back, reaching around her body for brief, forceful caresses. She was breathing rapidly, her heart beating from the exertion of the dance's steps ... and also from a feeling that she was finding harder to repress. Zarl's rough love play was getting to her.

Abruptly the music stopped, ripping away any false illusion that sensuous dancing was as far as the situation was supposed to go. Zarl's face now showed no uncertainty, and he pushed Helena toward a pile of cushions with purposeful strength.

Before Koenig could take the first irresistible stride to intervene, he heard an urgent whisper of breath from Tony. Looking back, he saw a dove come gliding in among the foliage to join the rest of the flock. The Vegans were all too occupied watching Zarl force Helena down on the cushions to notice the dull, misty blue that evolved into Maya.

Quietly she padded over and spoke in Koenig's ear. "I managed to get to the computer by flying over the top of the shield ... it's less effective the farther from the floor it gets."

Koenig frowned with impatience, waiting to hear what she had done to the computer that would stop the Vegans ... before it was too late.

Even in a whisper, Maya's voice conveyed regret as she explained. "The computer has a protective program that is intrinsic to its existence ... impossible to cancel or override. If any of its functions is disturbed, the stabilizers of its energy stores cease operating. The whole city would be blown out of existence."

Desperately Koenig asked, "What can we do, then? I can't stand any more of this!"

"The only way is to attack the weakest link. If we can malfunction one of the androids, then they all should shut down ... including the computer."

Tony had moved over to listen and snapped his fingers.

154

"Like the old Christmas tree lights! When one bulb goes out, it breaks the circuit and they all go out."

"What do we do, then? Use a stun-gun?" asked Koenig, not daring to look behind him to see how far things had developed between Zarl and Helena.

"No!" Tony warned urgently. "It won't work on androids. Besides, once they see a stunner in action they'll get the information they need. Their computer resources would enable it to duplicate and distribute them to all the androids in a matter of minutes."

In the silence of desperate deliberation, Koenig heard a low moan. It stopped only to sound again as a cry of arousal, and he knew Helena was no longer in control of herself. With a roar of hatred he turned and ran toward Zarl.

With calm expectation, Zarl rose up from the gasping Helena and waited for Koenig to reach him. Maya's shout of warning was to no avail as Koenig used the force of his charge behind a full roundhouse punch. It crashed into Zarl's jaw and made him stagger backwards.

The victorious Zamara rushed between them, laughing with success. Koenig was far more amazed at Zarl's reaction . . . now the steam of his jealousy had been partially relieved. The Vegan had absorbed the punch without a blink, only tripping backwards because of the effect of inertia. There was no sign of having felt any pain or being in the least in danger of passing out.

"You have seen!" Zamara shouted to the circle of androids. "You have been shown! Now kill them!"

The group of innocent-faced Vegans began to practice the blow that Koenig had thrown, taking turns belting each other in the jaw. None of them seemed in the least damaged, and the sounds of impact became louder as they rapidly developed a proficiency.

Zarl's analysis of the action was far quicker, since he had actually received the blow. He raised up his fist and stepped toward Koenig with scowling menace. As Koenig backed around the other side of a sturdy wooden table, Zarl decided to clear his path and practice the punch at the same time. With pure, robot strength he drove his knuckles into the tabletop, and it shattered like matchsticks.

Koenig leaped backwards, and Zarl bore down on him, stalking with the same certainty he had shown toward Helena ... but with a much different purpose. Then she leaped between them, placing herself perilously close to Zarl's cocked right arm.

"Zarl," she said gently, "please don't ..."

The effect on the android was far greater than that of Koenig's attack. His eyes blinked with confusion and distress.

"You don't have to be one of them any more," Helena continued. "You can be yourself ... think for yourself ... all you have to do is *choose* to."

Strong feeling swirled through Zarl in a blinding confusion. He felt rods of pain shooting across his brain, followed close behind by sensations of mellow peacefulness. The group collective consciousness immediately drove in on him to strangle him back into obedience, but their force was too great. Like an excessive grasp on a wet bar of soap, his persona shot out of their clutches and rose in its own flight of displacement.

Zamara shouted in panic, "Kill her, Zarl! Kill her!"

Helena's voice was still pleasantly urging. "You just have to take one more step to know what it is that we feel. You can become human."

Koenig stepped quickly to Helena's side, putting his arm affectionately around her. "Zarl," he said with a comradely smile, "I can see that you've got compassion. Now you want to feel love. You can! See us and you can feel it yourself."

Zamara had started to run over with the intention of killing the Alphans herself but there was a flare of heat inside her head that dropped her to her knees in pain. "Don't you see what they're doing, Zarl?" she screamed. "Stop it, Zarl! No! No!"

"It's your *own* choice, Zarl," Koenig persuaded. "Zamara is wrong. Love is strength, too. Take the final step ... take it and see!"

Both despair and delight surged through Zarl's mind,

156

and he could no longer understand which of his loyalties gave him which. Slowly he brought down his violence-poised arms and stretched them out. Inch by inch they crept around Helena and John, surrounding them with a circle of strength that could easily apply itself to squeeze them to a pulp.

"Don't stay a machine," Helena smiled, "become human."

Zarl's hands touched them, and for a split second he smiled back, his face creasing with the most natural and instinctive expression of friendship possible. Then his eyes closed, and he collapsed to the floor.

A great tide of change flowed through the garden, invisible but powerful. The sophisticated lighting blinked out, and harsh emergency bulbs came on. The foliage sagged, the leaves noticeably starting to wilt and the flowers to lose their brilliance. The temperature of the air slipped several degrees.

"What is it? What's happening?" Koenig asked.

Maya nodded approval. "It's all right," she said. "The master computer just shut down. There must be some kind of basic auxiliary system that's taken over."

Helena was kneeling beside Zarl, who stared past her into space, lost in wonder at an experience he could not explain. The other androids had ceased functioning immediately, frozen into frantic poses and looking like nothing more than beautifully shaped dummies.

"You were right," Zarl said softly as he focused on Helena. "I did feel it."

"I'm sorry, Zarl," Helena said with a sob. "I'm sorry."

"Please, don't feel sorry. It was worth it . . . that one . . . moment of . . . humanity."

The face of Zarl stiffened and sealed over with a glaze of inanimation. His functions ceased forever. Looking down at him, Koenig couldn't stop himself from wishing, in spite of everything, that the Vegan had survived.

It was not necessary to tell the numbers what had happened, and they came filing slowly into the grove with tears of gratitude streaking their faces. The hateful

157

masks were cast off at last, and they quickly set to work shifting the mechanical scrap of the androids out of sight.

Koenig unhooked his comlock from his belt and tried calling the Moon Base.

"Alpha to Commander Koenig," came the immediate reply from Yasko. "Moon Base functioning fully again."

"Glad to hear it," Koenig said. "Can you get an Eagle down here to pick us up?"

"Right away, Commander. Alpha out."

The air in the grove was getting cooler all the time. The luxurious environment that the master computer had kept operating was running down rapidly, and the Alphans' breaths were coming out in steamy puffs.

The numbers—the reinstated humans—seemed too pleased by their liberation to feel uncomfortable. Number 8 beamed his thanks at Koenig.

"What will you do now?" the Commander asked.

"We will live on the surface, as our ancestors did." The man laughed with joy at the prospect. "The climate is terribly harsh. It will be a struggle to survive. We'll have to learn to hunt and farm—it'll be wonderful!"

Helena blew on her chilled fingertips, not relishing the sound of that future at all. She had been told that the whole surface was covered in constant snow and that the winds seldom dropped below one hundred miles per hour.

She was surprised as her hands were grasped by Koenig, enclosing them with the warmth of his own. "That Zarl was quite some robot..."

Guardedly, she agreed.

"He was good-looking, aggressively masculine..." Koenig continued.

"He did have some very nice qualities."

The Commander's face immediately looked peeved that she had been led to confess a favorable opinion... even though he had done the leading himself. "Is that a testimonial?" he asked brusquely.

Helena laughed. "Just a statement of fact."

"If you prefer to put it that way..."

Helena's hands slipped out of his and up his arms

158

as she pulled to make him lean down closer to her. "I prefer an imperfect human being," she said pointedly.

Koenig felt inwardly warmed by the sentiment, understanding how it was really meant. He still looked stern, however, as he asked, "Is that your idea of a compliment?"

The sudden and welcoming roar of a distant Eagle's jets interrupted the conversation. They both grinned with anticipation, knowing they would soon be back home . . . on Alpha.